Smollets was down below, hunkered behind his horse's carcass. The horse was covered in blood. Smollets must have whipped him to death when he couldn't go on.

Slocum felt his blood begin to boil. If Smollets had known what the hell he was doing, that horse could have lasted him years and years. And now he'd died for Smollets, died for a homicidal son of a bitch who didn't give a shit about his horse or anybody or anything else.

Slocum kept his head low and sited his long gun on Smollets's head, which kept bobbing down below the horse's rib cage and out of sight.

Slocum took a deep breath, more to get control of himself than anything else. After Smollets's head disappeared once again, Slocum sited the place where it had been before. His target was a long way off—nearly four hundred yards, to the best of his reckoning—but Slocum was sure he could hit the murdering son of a bitch.

At least, if there was a God upstairs in heaven, he could . . .

DON'T MISS THESE
ALL-ACTION WESTERN SERIES
FROM THE BERKLEY PUBLISHING GROUP

THE GUNSMITH by J. R. Roberts

Clint Adams was a legend among lawmen, outlaws, and ladies. They called him . . . the Gunsmith.

LONGARM by Tabor Evans

The popular long-running series about Deputy U.S. Marshal Custis Long—his life, his loves, his fight for justice.

SLOCUM by Jake Logan

Today's longest-running action Western. John Slocum rides a deadly trail of hot blood and cold steel.

BUSHWHACKERS by B. J. Lanagan

An action-packed series by the creators of Longarm! The rousing adventures of the most brutal gang of cutthroats ever assembled—Quantrill's Raiders.

DIAMONDBACK by Guy Brewer

Dex Yancey is Diamondback, a Southern gentleman turned con man when his brother cheats him out of the family fortune. Ladies love him. Gamblers hate him. But nobody pulls one over on Dex . . .

WILDGUN by Jack Hanson

The blazing adventures of mountain man Will Barlow— from the creators of Longarm!

TEXAS TRACKER by Tom Calhoun

J.T. Law: the most relentless—and dangerous—manhunter in all Texas. Where sheriffs and posses fail, he's the best man to bring in the most vicious outlaws—for a price.

JAKE LOGAN

SLOCUM
AND THE
RUSTLER ON THE RUN

Yolo County Library
Woodland, CA 95695

J

JOVE BOOKS, NEW YORK

THE BERKLEY PUBLISHING GROUP
Published by the Penguin Group
Penguin Group (USA) Inc.
375 Hudson Street, New York, New York 10014, USA

Penguin Group (Canada), 90 Eglinton Avenue East, Suite 700, Toronto, Ontario M4P 2Y3, Canada
(a division of Pearson Penguin Canada Inc.)
Penguin Books Ltd., 80 Strand, London WC2R 0RL, England
Penguin Group Ireland, 25 St. Stephen's Green, Dublin 2, Ireland (a division of Penguin Books Ltd.)
Penguin Group (Australia), 250 Camberwell Road, Camberwell, Victoria 3124, Australia
(a division of Pearson Australia Group Pty. Ltd.)
Penguin Books India Pvt. Ltd., 11 Community Centre, Panchsheel Park, New Delhi—110 017, India
Penguin Group (NZ), 67 Apollo Drive, Rosedale, North Shore 0632, New Zealand
(a division of Pearson New Zealand Ltd.)
Penguin Books (South Africa) (Pty.) Ltd., 24 Sturdee Avenue, Rosebank, Johannesburg 2196,
South Africa

Penguin Books Ltd., Registered Offces: 80 Strand, London WC2R 0RL, England

This is a work of fiction. Names, characters, places, and incidents either are the product of the author's
imagination or are used fictitiously, and any resemblance to actual persons, living or dead, business
establishments, events, or locales is entirely coincidental.

SLOCUM AND THE RUSTLER ON THE RUN

A Jove Book / published by arrangement with the author

PRINTING HISTORY
Jove edition / August 2009

Copyright © 2009 by Penguin Group (USA) Inc.
Cover illustration by Sergio Giovine.

All rights reserved.
No part of this book may be reproduced, scanned, or distributed in any printed or electronic form without
permission. Please do not participate in or encourage piracy of copyrighted materials in violation of the
author's rights. Purchase only authorized editions.
For information, address: The Berkley Publishing Group,
a division of Penguin Group (USA) Inc.,
375 Hudson Street, New York, New York 10014.

ISBN: 978-0-515-14662-2

JOVE®
Jove Books are published by The Berkley Publishing Group,
a division of Penguin Group (USA) Inc.
375 Hudson Street, New York, New York 10014.
JOVE® is a registered trademark of Penguin Group (USA) Inc.
The "J" design is a trademark of Penguin Group (USA) Inc.

PRINTED IN THE UNITED STATES OF AMERICA

10 9 8 7 6 5 4 3 2 1

If you purchased this book without a cover, you should be aware that this book is stolen property. It
was reported as "unsold and destroyed" to the publisher, and neither the author nor the publisher has
received any payment for this "stripped book."

1

After riding out from Hiram Walker's cattle ranch near Tucson, Slocum and his companions headed northwest, their trail heading them for Lonesome, California. Lonesome was the town in which Goose Martin, one of Slocum's friends, had lost his brother and nephew, murdered in a night-darkened alley by Slocum. Or so Goose had been told.

He'd tracked Slocum all over California, Nevada, and Arizona until he'd finally run him down north of Tucson—and been convinced of Slocum's innocence not only by Slocum's nature, but by the hard evidence provided by telegrams from the Lonesome sheriff and the livery owner, among others.

Slocum hadn't ridden into Lonesome until after the deaths, had stayed one day, then ridden out.

Well, Goose hadn't had all that much faith in his witnesses in the first place, to tell the truth. He had gotten most of it from two youngish fellas over at the saloon, and now he figured they must have been drunk or lying. Maybe both.

But Slocum had promised to help him find his family's

killers. And Slocum, Goose was fast learning, was a man of his word. And more. He had found Hiram Walker's rustlers— plus a mess of other ranchers' thieved cattle—and when the other owners began turning up to press money on him, he'd shared it with them, even though they hadn't expected it, hadn't whispered a word! Plus, he was sharing the reward money for the thieves. The Tucson sheriff would be wiring that shortly.

All in all, Goose was mighty grateful that he'd run into Slocum, no matter what the circumstance, because Slocum had also given him a son—the third man in their party. A son he hadn't known existed.

Born of an El Paso whore, young Xander could just as easily have been Slocum's boy, and had passed for it for a while. Goose figured Slocum had been relieved and bereft, all at the same time, to give him over.

But still, he had. And Goose had to admire that. Even Xander had insisted on being fathered by Slocum, on ac- count of his mother had told him so. He'd read every single book written about Slocum—and there were plenty—and had wanted to meet him since he was in diapers. But Slocum's theory of Goose's fatherhood—and not his— convinced Xander, too.

Goose was glad, exceedingly glad. Now he had a fine, handsome, strapping son to add to his family of a wife and three daughters—each just as redheaded and green-eyed as Xander.

So now Goose would return home to Seattle with a son, a sack full of money, and having taken care of his brother and nephew's killer or killers. He hoped that afterward, Slocum could be convinced to go along home with him and stay for at least a while. Mariska, Goose's Russian wife, would be honored to meet him, and he knew that Xander would likely be more comfortable. They both had the high- est regards for the man.

* * *

They made camp for the night just on the western side of the Colorado River, in California. It had taken them three days to make it that far, and Goose's immediate destination was a good bit farther north—nearly to Sacramento. It was a long trip, but Slocum was enjoying the company. He'd talked to Goose at length about the killings and the "witnesses" who had put themselves forth, and he already had a fairly good idea of where to start.

He felt good, too, about having left Harvey Smollets far behind. He hoped. He seemed to find somebody with a new vendetta for him at every place he stopped, and Hiram Walker's ranch had been no different. Smollets had been a neighbor and, ultimately, the head cattle thief.

Just after his arrest, there had been an altercation, during which he'd killed the old woman who was feeding the prisoners in the Tucson jail during the sheriff's absence. And, not incidentally, emptied the jail of prisoners.

Only one had not escaped, and that was only because he came back voluntarily. He was the youngest of Smollets's recruits, Milo Herrick, and his only part in the thefts was to feed and water the stock before Smollets "corrected" the brands and integrated them into his herd.

Slocum had spoken about him with the sheriff before he and the Martins left for California, and Sheriff Black was convinced the judge would go easy on him. Slocum was pleased.

The one thing he wasn't too happy about—as far as leaving the Territory was concerned—was, with it, leaving Samantha behind. She was Hiram's cook, and a pure-D wonder at it. Among other things more personal—and more vital—to a fellow of Slocum's tastes.

But Sam was far behind him by this time, and wishing for her didn't put her with him, so he tried to eradicate those particular yearnings from his mind. Instead, he tried to focus on where they were going and why, and who had killed Goose's brother and his nephew.

And when he got tired of thinking about that, there was also Xander to ponder. He had really hated to give up his claim to the boy's paternity, more so with each passing day, it seemed to him. Xander was a fine boy with lots of potential, and if Goose hadn't happened along—and turned out to have been with Xander's mother just a week or so prior to Slocum—well . . . Slocum would most likely be headed back east, to get the boy set up in a school. A good school.

But Xander wasn't his, he kept reminding himself, no matter how much he wished things were different. Goose would make a good father to him, and if Slocum had to lose the boy, he couldn't have picked a better candidate to take over for him.

"We still got any of that cake left from Hiram's?" Goose asked, jarring Slocum out of his reverie.

"No," he said. "Think Xander polished that off this noontime."

Xander had the good sense to look a little guilty. "Sorry, Pa," he said to Goose. "'Fraid most'a the stuff Miss Samantha packed up for us is all gone. Sure was good, though, wasn't it?"

Goose, who knew a little more about Slocum's dalliance with Hiram's cook than did the boy, said, "I'll bet Slocum's gonna go back for more, once he gets round to it."

Slocum grunted, acknowledging the comment, then pulled his saddlebags closer. "Think I got some old jerky and hardtack in here. Reckon it'll do for now." After Sam's fried chicken and potato salad, ham sandwiches, and a bevy of desserts, jerky and hardtack didn't seem fit for human consumption. But he pulled out the jerky anyhow.

Goose reached for the hardtack, gnawed off a corner, and said, "Man . . ."

"Exactly," said Slocum in agreement, and jammed the jerky in his mouth.

"Remind me to shoot some game tomorrow," Xander said, and reluctantly joined Goose in the hardtack.

* * *

Much nearer than Slocum would have liked—a mere twenty miles to the south, as a matter of fact—a lone man had stopped for the night, too.

He was in the process of building a small fire. Not for cooking, but to keep the animals away. He didn't care for food tonight, or coffee. He just wanted to sleep safely, and not to wake to find himself being eaten by a Mexican grizzly.

He was Harvey Smollets by name, and by trade he was a fairly good cattle rustler, a poor card cheat, and fair to mediocre at any number of the underhanded ploys used by men of dubious morals to make their way in the West.

He had been run out of England by his family and paid to stay in the States. Which had been fine, as long as they were alive. But they were all dead now, and Harvey had already used up what would have been his inheritance. His, and his sister's, as well.

The fire finally burned steadily, and he sat back, inside the ring of rope he'd already laid down as a rattlesnake precaution. What a land this was, where one had to guard oneself from the fangs and claws of creatures that in another time and place would have been either friendly or nonexistent, or would have run from the scent and sound of man.

Things were always better in another time or place, so far as Harvey Smollets was concerned.

A coyote howled, and he hugged his legs, shivering despite the warm night.

2

Four days, one thrown horseshoe, seven rabbits, and twice as many desert quail later, the tired trio at last rode into Lonesome. Goose, of course, wanted to get to the detecting part right off the bat, but Slocum favored getting Xander's horse reshod, and packing away a good restaurant meal.

Nobody argued very hard against it.

They ate a substantial meal at Aunt Ruby's Café—steak with all the trimmings, plus apple pie, plus her special chocolate cake—and it being dark by the time they were finished, they figured now would be a choice time to wander over to the Branchwater Saloon—the place where Goose had talked to those cowhands who'd identified Slocum as the killer in the first place. Slocum hoped the two sonsabitches would still be hanging around.

If they were local, there was a good chance of it, he figured.

When they entered the Branchwater, it appeared a quiet, fairly normal town drinking hole. Nothing special about it. The usual prints of naked ladies hung on the dusty walls, along with a few old wanted posters and framed photographs of local big shots, the mayor and so on.

Judging by the old wanted posters, Slocum could easily figure out how his name had come to trip off the locals' tongues so easily. He was the featured outlaw in at least three of them.

He grabbed Goose and hauled him over to the wall, saying, "I think I know where they got the idea."

Goose scratched his head as Slocum began ripping down the old paper. "Well, I'll be jiggered!"

Under his breath Slocum muttered, "Charges dropped," at the first poster, "Charges dropped," at the second, and "Stupid bastards!" at the third.

Goose's mouth crooked up into a smile. "Stupid bastards?"

Slocum wadded the posters up and tossed them into a trash bag on the floor. "Stupid sheriff, inept deputy, hollow-brained victim, blind-as-a-bat eyewitness, idiot—"

Goose held up his hands, cutting Slocum off. "I get the picture. Stupid bastards, right?"

Slocum gave him a curt nod. "Right." And then, at the barkeep's approach, he brightened. "Bourbon and branch," he said. "The same for you, Goose?"

While Goose was nodding, Xander piped up, "Make it three."

At a quizzical look from Slocum, the boy shrugged. "Hiram didn't have any branchwater," he explained.

"Doubt they do here, either," Slocum said, grinning. The boy seemed bound and determined to sample every sort of alcoholic beverage available, just to see what he liked and disliked. Judging by the past outcomes, Slocum figured Xander would mark the bourbon and branch on the "dislike" side of the scale.

But Xander fooled him, and had put away enough bourbon and branch in the next three hours to make him stagger back to the hotel and get lost twice trying to navigate to the outhouse.

Once they had the boy passed out on his mattress, Goose looked at Slocum and said, "Believe he's found somethin' he likes."

"He'd best stop likin' it quite so much," Slocum replied with a shake of his head. "He showed too big a money roll at the bar when he was payin' his tab. Best have him watch that, or he's liable to end up like his uncle and cousin."

Goose nodded. "Was gonna mention that to him in the mornin'."

Slocum grunted softly. "You ready to go back?" he asked.

Goose arched a sandy brow. "Go back? Back where? To the bar?"

"Where else?"

Goose let out a sigh, then walked forward, indicating his reluctant approval. As they went down the stairs to the hotel lobby, Slocum said, "I wanna talk to some more of those fellas."

They tramped back up to the saloon, and when they arrived, there were several newcomers at the bar. Goose stopped, then nudged him. "They're here," he said.

"Which ones?" asked Slocum, scanning the crowd.

"Halfway down the bar. Feller in the checkered shirt and the younger one beside him, in the buckskin jacket." Goose snorted in excitement.

Slocum put a restraining hand on his arm. "Don't go gunnin' anybody down, yet. Get us a table."

While Goose reluctantly sat down nearby, Slocum sauntered down the bar, toward the checkered shirt and the buckskin jacket. There was a space next to the checkered shirt, who turned out to be a light-brown-headed fellow of about thirty-five, with bad, pockmarked skin and dark eyes.

"Howdy," Slocum said casually. "Name's Slocum." He stuck out his hand.

The man didn't take it. He did turn his head toward Slocum, though, and said, "Evenin'." Then he looked Slocum up and down. "Been travelin'?"

Slocum nodded, and retracted his hand before he noticed the barkeep waiting. "Beer," he said. Then he smiled at the man with the pockmarked skin. "Washes down the dust."

The bartender slid a large mug of beer in front of him, and Slocum slapped twenty-five cents down on the bar top. The man had turned away from him, although he wasn't engaged in conversation with his little friend in the fringed jacket, who had curly black hair and blue eyes, and looked to be about twenty or so. They made an odd pair.

Slocum tapped Checkered Shirt on the shoulder. When the man turned his face Slocum's way, Slocum said, "Didn't catch your name, friend."

Checkered Shirt smiled a little, then said, "Didn't throw it," before he turned away again. The boy in the fringed jacket thought this was pretty funny, and snorted beer all over the bar in front of him.

"Knock it off, Tim," snapped the barkeep, who mopped the bar with a towel.

Tim. Well, at least Slocum had one name. But he wanted more than that.

"Tim!" he barked jovially. Well, semi-jovially, anyway. He was growing weary of these two. "Want to ask you some questions. Like, for instance, what you were up to on the evening of . . ." He slid a look toward Goose, who held up fingers to indicate the month and day. ". . . on the evening of March 16. See anything different that night? Anything out of the ordinary?"

The boy stared at him, blinking. "Huh?" he finally said.

Goose was getting as antsy as Slocum was peeved. Why didn't Slocum want him over there, anyhow? Why didn't he just slug ol' Checkered Shirt right in the center of that ugly mug of his? Goose would have. He would have done it five minutes ago!

Now he understood why Slocum had wanted to drop Xander back at the hotel before he got down to serious questioning. He didn't want the kid to see what a wuss he really was. No, that couldn't be it. He'd seen Slocum under a whole lot more pressure than those two yahoos at the bar were providing, and it just rolled off his back.

So why was he acting this way?

So . . . *nice*?

Goose put his hand on the table and prepared to stand up. He'd give those two cowhands what for, or his name wasn't Goose Martin!

The brown-haired man in the checkered shirt finally introduced himself after a bit more goading from Tim. "Name's Hobbins," he said, without a smile. "Roy Hobbins."

"Good to meet you, Hobbins," Slocum said. "Now, if you fellas could just give me a clue as to what you were doin' that evenin'?"

Hobbins arched a brow. "Why?"

"Because my buddy's brother and nephew got killed that night," Slocum said, "and accordin' to him, you two boys saw it."

"Oh sure!" Tim piped up. "In the alley! We seen practically the whole thing, didn't we, Roy?"

Roy Hobbins gave a curt nod, but said not a word.

"Well, I wonder if you could tell me the story. I have kind of a different way of lookin' at things than my buddy does." Slocum took a drink of his beer.

"We seen 'em earlier, in here," Tim volunteered. "We left a few minutes after they did."

"What were they doin'? Were they playin' cards or just drinkin'?" Slocum asked, focusing on the boy.

"Just drinkin'," Tim said. "They was at the bar."

Slocum nodded just as Goose joined them.

Hobbins glanced up at Goose and said, "Yeah. I remember you. Told you—and the sheriff—everythin' I seen, already. You're called Duck or somethin', ain't you."

"Goose," Goose said, under his breath. Slocum noticed that he kept on balling his hands into fists over and over.

Slocum put a hand on his shoulder, hoping it would calm him—or at least signal him to back the hell off. He wanted to do this his way. He said, "Sorry to make you repeat yourselves, fellas, but I just wanna get the facts first-hand, and you're the only firsthand witnesses."

It had the desired effect. Tim stood up a little taller, and Hobbins's demeanor took on a bit of an air of authority. Hobbins said, "Just like the kid, here, said, we left a few minutes after they did and started up toward the livery. We wanted to get back to the ranch before midnight, and it was a full moon. Decent for ridin'."

"And that was at about what time?" Slocum interjected.

"'Bout eight-thirty," Hobbins said, and Tim nodded, concurring.

Slocum grunted. He asked, "So you were walking to the livery—that the same direction as the hotel?"

"Yup," said Hobbins.

"And then?"

"We come up to the mouth of the second alley—" Tim started, but Hobbins cut him off.

"Shut up and lemme tell it," Hobbins snapped at the younger man.

Tim took a step back, out of Hobbins's swinging range.

Hobbins went on. "We was just coming up to the alley by Grant's Mercantile when we heard the first shot, then seen a man back his way out—barely out—of the alley's mouth. Just one step. And then he fired again."

"You see his face?"

"Nope. Just his backside. We was flat against the wall, so he didn't even see us. He just took off runnin' the other way, jumped on a horse tied at the rail out front of Grant's Mercantile, and he was gone. That's it."

"Did you find the bodies?" Slocum asked, trying to pump for more information.

Tim opened his mouth, although he took yet another step back from Hobbins before he did it. "They was down in the alley, shot in the back, both of 'em. The dust was still eddyin' up a mite from where they fell."

Goose spoke once more, before Slocum had a chance. "And they were both dead?" His voice cracked with emotion.

"Yeah, dead as a couple of hammers," said Hobbins. "I sent the boy runnin' for the sheriff."

Tim nodded and said, "Sorry," to Goose, as if he'd said it before. Which he probably had, Slocum figured.

He asked, "What color horse did he jump on? Was it his, or just one he grabbed, random-like?"

Hobbins shrugged his shoulders. "Don't know whose it was. Likely his, though. Sheriff didn't say nothin' about horse thievin'."

"It was a fancy-colored horse," added Tim. "One'a them Palouse ponies, you know? Speckled on the rump end."

Hobbins nodded. "Rest of it was chestnut or sorrel, I reckon. Too dark to tell for sure."

"Good, good," Slocum said, nodding. "Just one last question and then we'll be done with you boys."

Hobbins nodded and waited.

"Why'd you tell Goose, here, that the killer was me?"

Hobbins raised his chin and eyebrows at the same time. "I ain't never seen you before in my life, mister!"

"That's why I asked you why," Slocum said, his face expressionless.

Goose was staring down Tim, who was looking fairly nervous. Goose said, "It was you who said the name. You're the one who told me it was Slocum."

"I just seen a poster on the wall!" the boy blurted. "He

just looked kinda like him, I mean, the build and stuff. I didn't see his face, either. Mr. Slocum?"

Slocum flicked his eyes over to Tim.

"Mr. Slocum, I'm awful sorry, real sorry. It's just that . . ."

Hobbins looked over at Goose. "I seem to remember you bein' awful pushy about askin' for information, mister. The kid prob'ly just gave the first name that came to mind. Just to make you go the hell away."

Goose sighed and dropped his gaze. Slocum knew Goose well enough to know that Hobbins was probably right—Goose could be pretty damned pushy when he had his mind set on something.

Slocum drained his beer and set the mug down on the counter. He stood erect. "Well, I thank you kindly for answerin' my questions, fellas. You've been a big help. Goose? Let's get back to the hotel. I wanna go see the sheriff soon's he opens in the morning."

Goose muttered, "Yup," then in a louder voice, added, "Yeah, thanks, fellas." He followed Slocum outside and up the walk.

When Slocum came to the mouth of the alley where the murders had taken place, he stopped and pressed Goose up against the building. "We got nigh on a full moon tonight," he said. "You tell me if you can see my face."

He disappeared into the alley, then stepped out, his back to the street, exactly one step. He held out his arm as if he were pointing a gun at someone or something farther down the alley.

"Nope," said a dejected Goose. "Can't see nothin' 'cept your shape."

Slocum turned toward him. "All right. Guess we can't do much more until tomorrow, when it's light."

But he wondered, as they walked back to the hotel, where that alley went, and why on earth Goose's brother and nephew would have been headed down it in the first place.

3

The next morning, Harvey Smollets was up with the dawn and already traveling toward the nearest town, a burg by the name of Lonesome.

He had spent a rough night, convinced that he was going to be attacked by gangs of snakes or bobcats or cougars or bears while he slept. And therefore, he slept very little. He had already decided that when he got to Lonesome, he would check into the hotel—if they had one—and spend a couple of nights before moving on again. His goal was San Francisco, but he figured that he'd prefer to make it awake.

And alive.

Slocum woke before Goose, and went about his morning routine quietly, trying not to wake him. That shot that Goose had taken in the back, out at Hiram Walker's ranch, had been meant for Slocum. And although Goose seemed to be a fast healer, it was still bothering him despite the extra time they'd taken at Hiram's. It seemed to be worse toward the end of the day. Slocum had practically had to carry him up the stairs when they came home for the final time.

By the time Slocum was ready to move out and go check the alley again, Goose was still sleeping, as was Xander. He still couldn't bring himself to disturb either one, so Slocum quietly let himself out into the hall and went down the stairs alone.

He nodded at the desk clerk on his way out, and walked over to the alley where Goose's relatives had met their maker. He stopped at the mouth of it and gave it a long looking over. No doorways, just barrels and a couple of crates.

Shrugging, he moved forward. The other end of the alley opened out onto another street, this one totally residential, which left him to scratch his head. Why the heck would they have traveled this route? The hotel clerk had told them last night that the men had been booked at the hotel, and he'd showed them the register to prove it. And the stable was only a half block farther than that, all on the main road.

He shook his head.

He started up the street, checking the names painted on the front gates or fences, trying to find something familiar. But there was nothing. Nothing that made sense to him, anyway. He'd have to have Goose come out and check, he decided. Maybe Goose would recognize somebody his brother would have known.

Slocum hiked back the way he'd come and headed toward the sheriff's office. It was a little early, but he supposed he could try.

In fact, the sheriff was already in his office, and was quite startled when Slocum walked in.

"Who the hell are you?!" he shouted, reaching for his sidearm.

Slocum immediately held up his hands, palms forward. "Good mornin' to you, too!" he said.

The sheriff holstered his gun and shook his head. "Sorry," he said. "Just ain't used to doin' no business this early of a mornin'. What can I do you for?"

"Mind?" asked Slocum, indicating the chair nearest him.

"Go 'head." The sheriff sat down behind the desk to face him.

"First of all, my name's Slocum. John Slocum."

The sheriff nodded. "Heard the name."

"You had a shootin' here in town not too long ago, and two fellas—Roy Hobbins and Tim Somethin'—identified me as the killer. Believe you got a wire a week or so ago from one Goose Martin, askin' for the dates I come in and outta town."

"That I did. Believe I cleared you." The sheriff smiled briefly.

"And thank you for that," Slocum replied with a nod. "Now I'm here in town with Goose Martin. He's the brother and uncle of the two men killed, and I've given my word I'll help him find the real culprit."

The sheriff nodded. "Name's Dodge, by the way. Wade Dodge."

They shook hands across the desk, then Sheriff Dodge went on. "I'm afraid you're gonna have a rough go of it. I ain't turned up clue one."

"Nothin' on who they talked to while they were in town? Why the hell they were walkin' down an alley toward a residential section when they got shot?"

One corner of the sheriff's mouth quirked up into a questioning yet curious half smile. "Been busy, ain't you?"

"Ain't hardly started yet," Slocum replied with a straight face.

After leaving Sheriff Dodge behind—and deciding he wasn't such a bad fellow, after all—Slocum walked down to the stable and took care of Speck, Eagle, and Kip, then hiked back to the hotel. He wanted those Martin boys up and at 'em, or he was gonna eat breakfast without them.

But before he made it all the way to the hotel, Xander popped out of a doorway just ahead of him. There was a red-checkered bib around his neck and a chunk of toasted bread in his hand, dribbling melted butter down his arm. "Mornin'!" he said.

Slocum read the sign on the door the kid had just popped out of. "Larkin's Café," it said.

"Goose in there with you?"

"He sure is. C'mon!" Xander grabbed hold of Slocum's sleeve. "Their breakfast is almost as good as Miss Samantha's!"

Slocum found that hard to believe, but he went inside anyway, and joined Goose and Xander at their table. They had picked one by the window, to keep an eye peeled for him, and had already been served. A waiter handed Slocum a menu.

He barely glanced at it. He jabbed a thumb toward Goose's plate and said, "I'll have what he's havin', but don't cook the beef so dang long. Leave some 'moo' in the middle." He handed back the menu, and the waiter fetched him some coffee, toast, bacon, and eggs to start with. Goose must've ordered a bigger breakfast than he'd thought.

Slocum wasn't going to argue with anybody about it, though. He immediately began to chow down on his food.

After topping off breakfast with three thick slices of cheddar-topped apple pie, the trio walked back up the street to the alley.

"Like I told you," Slocum began, "ain't nothin' but houses beyond. But maybe there's a name you'd recognize, somebody your brother would have talked about sometime. All the houses ain't got folks' names, but—"

"Live in hope?" Xander butted in.

Slocum sighed. "Yeah." He was tired, and full as a tick. So he walked them through the alley, sat down on a packing crate, and swept his arm toward the street. "Have at it," he said. He leaned back against the building and closed his eyes.

* * *

Slocum awoke from his catnap with a start—somebody was about to shake his arm off.

He opened his eyes to find that Xander was the culprit, and excited was too mild a word for his current condition. "Slocum! Slocum! Wake up, Slocum!"

Slocum gently swatted him away and stretched out his arms. He didn't know how long he'd been catnapping, but it must have been a while. He had a hell of a kink in his neck. He rubbed at it, wincing, then said, "Calm down, boy. What's so important?"

"Ezra Noonan," said the boy, and pointed to a little whitewashed house down the street. "Ezra Noonan lives there," he repeated, as if Slocum should know what he was talking about.

Slocum didn't have a clue, and he shook his head.

Xander took a gulp of air and plunged in, "Ezra Noonan knew my pa and uncle Bill when they were little kids, so don't you see? Uncle Bill and Badger were on their way to visit Ezra, which was why they was headed down the alley in the first place! Pa's talkin' with him now, and wonders could you come down and meet him."

Slocum, imagining a grizzled old man who likely couldn't figure out who the hell Goose was, hopped down off the packing crate and, rubbing his sore neck, said, "All right, Xander, lead the way."

When they got down to Ezra Noonan's house, Xander pounded on the front door a few times before Goose answered it and ushered them both inside. "Sorry to make you come, Slocum, but I figured you might be interested in what Ezra had to say."

Slocum nodded and thanked Goose, while Goose led them down the hall to the kitchen.

There, in the morning sunshine pouring through the kitchen windows, stood a man with his back to them. He was of medium height and well dressed, and had neatly barbered hair—not silver, but dark brown, lightly salted with gray. He turned around to face them, and proved to be Goose's senior by only about ten years. He smiled a bit, and said, "And this is Mr. Slocum, I assume?"

Slocum took a few steps forward and stuck out his hand. "It's just Slocum, Mr. Noonan."

Noonan took his hand and shook it, saying, "Call me Ezra, Slocum, please."

Slocum nodded. "Ezra, Xander here tells me that Goose figures his brother and nephew were on their way to visit you when they were killed."

Ezra lowered his head and shook it slowly. "I'm afraid that's most likely the case. Poor Bill. I was so wanting to meet his son." He brightened slightly. "But I've met yours, Goose."

Xander grinned. "Sure have, Mr. Noonan."

Ezra returned his smile, although weakly. "I went to see Sheriff Dodge. He was no help at all."

"Funny," muttered Slocum. "Didn't mention a damn thing about it when I was up there."

"Our sheriff is a tight-lipped man," Ezra said, as if he were disgusted with the whole affair. Then he held his arm toward the kitchen table. "Forgive my manners. Please sit down, gentlemen."

Slocum pulled out a chair while Goose and Xander did the same. "Don't mind if I do." Then he looked up at Ezra. "You seem like a real clear-spoken man. Did they write to tell you they was comin', or had they been here before?"

"No, never before. I'm actually back from Chicago. Retired." Slocum must have made a face, because Ezra continued, "My father sent me back east from Kansas City—that's where the Martin boys and I grew up—when I was about thirteen, almost fourteen, to go to school. I ended up staying until I moved to Chicago about ten years ago. Cattle buyer. And when I retired, I left the snow and the wind behind and came home to California." He pulled out the chair at the table's head and sat down.

"They wrote," he went on. "Let me tell you, I was surprised to hear from old Bill after so many years! All grown up, his wife gone, and with a son. But of course, he would be all grown up, but I had him in my head as an eleven-year-old, you know?" He shook his head. "Time plays tricks with the memory, I suppose. I saw them at the undertaker's before the services. I think, if he had knocked at my door with no warning, I would have recognized Bill, though. Still had that hair, as red as a fox's pelt, and he was big like you, Goose. Like your father was."

Slocum noticed that Goose was wiping away a tear, and looked away, choosing not to see it. This family had enough troubles without him pointing it out. Xander seemed to be holding up pretty well, though.

Slocum supposed it helped that Xander had never met his uncle or his cousin. And now he never would.

4

They spent the better part of the day with Ezra Noonan. Slocum doled out the questions, and Ezra answered to the best of his ability. Goose seemed comfortable with him, and in fact seemed to take everything he said as if it were the word of God.

Xander grew restless, though, but he calmed down when lunchtime came around, and packed away three thick beef sandwiches—with cheddar—and two tall glasses of limeade.

The kid was a bottomless pit.

Still, with all his questions and Ezra's answers, Slocum was no closer to finding Bill and Badger's killers. He had asked if they were in town long enough to have made any enemies.

No.

Did they mention that they were being trailed by anyone, for any reason?

No. Again, Ezra hadn't seen them, only heard from them by letter.

Ezra produced the letter, and Slocum read it. Not clue one, except that Bill couldn't spell worth beans.

Slocum finally had to admit defeat.

He excused himself at about three in the afternoon, left Goose and Xander behind to continue catching up, and made his way back through the alley and down to the livery again.

The hostler, Mick Trace, was present this time, and Slocum began grilling him. He had no information, either, and Slocum was beginning to wonder if anybody in this godforsaken town had eyes or ears.

He walked back up to the sheriff's office and quizzed the sheriff about Ezra's inquiry.

"Did I forget to mention that?" he asked. "He was in here the next mornin'. Said they were on their way to visit him and never showed."

Slocum sat back in his chair and thoughtfully tapped his lips with a finger. "You know if they talked to anybody else while they were in town? Had an argument, anything like that?"

The sheriff shook his head. "They was perfect town guests. Didn't make so much as a ripple."

"Except for gettin' murdered."

The sheriff snorted. "Yeah, well, there's that . . ."

Slocum shoved his chair back with a scrape. "All right. Won't bother you no more." He stood and went to the door. "'Less, of course, there was anybody else you forgot to mention the first time."

"Only Bob Carter, but his statement don't amount to much."

"Can I see it?"

Slocum waited while the sheriff dug through his filing cabinet and found the folder, then handed it to Slocum.

"Who's Carter?" Slocum asked, accepting the folder.

"He was at the bar that night," Sheriff Dodge said. "Seen the Martins leave, seen Roy and Tim leave a few minutes later. That's it."

Slocum nodded and opened the folder. And that was, indeed, it. Carter's statement didn't even take up a quarter of a page.

Slocum handed it back, shaking his head, and bade the sheriff good-bye.

As he walked back down the street, Slocum's mind raced. If the Martins had made no enemies during their short stay in town, then that left two possibilities: either somebody with a grudge had tracked them into town, or they'd been victims of mistaken identity.

Slocum was evenly divided between the two scenarios.

He stopped into the saloon and stepped up to the bar. The place was the next thing to deserted, there being only two other customers besides Slocum.

The bartender faced him across the bar. "What can I get you?"

"Whiskey," Slocum said, and when the barkeep returned with it, he asked, "Were you workin' the night that those strangers got shot in the alley up the way?"

"Yup," the bartender replied. "Feller don't forget a thing like that, no sir. Why you ask?"

"They were brother and nephew to a friend of mine. Anything odd happen that night, while they were in the bar? They get in an argument with somebody? Anything like that?"

The barkeep shook his head. "No, they was real quiet. Kept to themselves, like. Both were drinkin' beer all evening, and they left early. Weren't liquored-up or nothin'."

"Was there another stranger in the bar that night? Somebody who might'a left around the time that they did?"

He gave a brief description—all the information he had—to the bartender.

The bartender scratched at his ear, then shook his head. "Not that I recall. And if a man's in here drinkin', I remember him."

Slocum nodded and took a draw on his beer. "Okay. You

remember anything more, you make sure and let me know. Name's Slocum, and I'm stayin' up the street at the hotel."

The barkeep nodded, then shrugged. "Sure thing. But I'm pretty sure I ain't gonna recall nothin' more."

Slocum finished his beer, taking his time, looking at the characters around the place, and when he was finished, he sauntered toward the batwing doors. He barely had them open when Tim, the kid from the night before, ran smack into him.

"Oh! Sorry!" said the boy, clutching at his heart. "I was lookin' for you, but didn't expect to find you right there!"

Slocum put a hand on the boy's shoulder. "It's all right, son. Just calm down. How come you're in such a rip-roarin' rush, anyhow?"

Still panting, the kid said, "It's Roy who's in a rush. You remember Roy? The feller I was with last night?"

Slocum nodded.

"Well, he remembered somethin' else. He said it probably wasn't nothin' important, but he thought we should tell you anyway. Are you the Slocum that them wanted posters was for?"

It was suddenly clear to Slocum. Roy Hobbins had recognized him from those old wanted posters, and now he was afraid to hold back any information that Slocum could possibly want. So much for all the bravado he'd put forth last night.

"Yeah, I'm that Slocum," he said, letting a little growl creep into his voice. He enjoyed the drama of it.

Tim quaked a little, but stood his ground.

"So, what did you two remember?"

"It was Roy," said the boy. "He remembered something that the killer said. When he was standin' in the alley."

Slocum nodded. "Tell me."

"We both heard it plain as day." The kid had stopped shaking and pulled himself up. "He just said one word.

Before he fired the second shot, I mean. Shit. I mean, that's what he said. 'Shit.'"

"Just the way you said it?"

Young Tim nodded. "Exactly like that."

Down the street, at the hotel, Harvey Smollets was just falling asleep. He'd pulled into town about an hour and a half ago, stabled his horse, grabbed some lunch, and checked into the hotel without scanning the register, and therefore didn't realize that Slocum, the man he'd tried to kill out at Hiram Walker's ranch, was checked into the room just down the hall from him.

He also didn't know that the man his bullet had hit, Goose Martin, was a guest in the hotel, too. It was hard to say what Smollets would have done if he'd known. On one hand, he was still mad enough at Slocum—whom he blamed for all of his current misfortune—to want to kill him. But then, he'd learned a bit about Slocum during his travels, and now had the good sense to be just a little afraid of him. Well, more than a little.

But Slocum was the furthest thing from his mind at the moment. All he was thinking about was the soft pillow and linens he lay on, the cool California breeze softly ruffling his curtains, and a long, uninterrupted rest.

Slocum hiked back over to the other street and down it to Ezra Noonan's house. A knock on the door proved that the Martins were still there—Xander opened the door.

"Hiya, Slocum!" he said. "Come to join us for some dinner?"

"I might be talked into it," Slocum replied, tousling the boy's hair as he crossed the threshold. The men had moved into the parlor by now, and Goose was laughing.

"Howdy, Slocum!" he said between guffaws, rising to his feet. "We was just talkin' 'bout old times. I swan, ol'

Ezra's got about the best head for rememberin' that I ever did run acrost in all my borned days!"

Ezra was laughing, too. He said, "You're not so bad yourself, Goose! I completely forgot about that time with the catfish!"

"The *giant* catfish!" Goose rejoined.

The three of them, including Xander, suddenly burst out into even more animated laughter and knee slapping. Slocum had to back up and sit down just to get out of the line of fire.

After dinner, and after the hilarity wore off, Slocum broke the unhappy news.

"And so," he said in conclusion, "I just don't see no way we can find the killer. I figure he was a professional, and realized his mistake too late. He's probably a couple hundred miles from here by now."

Goose's head sank into his hands. "Christ, they was killed by accident?"

Ezra said, "There can be no doubt, Slocum?"

"Not the way I see it," Slocum replied. "If anybody else thinks different, speak up and we'll start again. But I'm sorry, Goose, really sorry. That's what I come up with."

Even Xander was broken up about it. Slocum supposed he'd been looking forward to witnessing a shoot-out of sorts. Slocum was halfway sorry to disappoint him.

After about a half hour, Goose was in control enough to take the walk back to the hotel, and they started out, Slocum propping up his arm. It was a good thing, because Goose was walking with his head down and paying no attention to where they were going.

Slocum said, "Goose, it's a tragic thing, losin' family to anything, let alone a mistake. But you did more than lose. You gained a son. A fine, strappin' son who'll always have your back."

Goose nodded. "Thanks, Slocum. I know. Thanks for

tryin', anyhow." He rubbed his face on his sleeve. "You done the best you could. If there's a hell, I hope that murderin' son of a bitch burns forever."

"I hear you, Goose," Slocum said in agreement. He looked around for Xander, and found that he'd gone ahead of them, up the alley. "What you say we stop in at the saloon for a good healthy shot of bourbon?" It was only eight and therefore early, and he figured if anybody deserved a good stiff drink, it was Goose.

Goose didn't answer him, so he took that for a yes and guided him up through the alley, calling up to Xander to detour to the saloon. By the time he and Goose made it, Xander already had a table staked out. Slocum deposited Goose in a chair, then made his way through the thin crowd, up to the bar.

"You got any good bourbon?" he asked. "And I mean good."

The barkeep looked around as if they were discussing a state secret, then whispered, "I got one bottle of Kentucky bourbon I been keepin' back for years. It's gonna cost you, though."

Slocum nodded. "Fine. I'll take it."

5

Xander, who'd held himself down to beer, helped Slocum get Goose back to the hotel and into bed, then Xander settled in, and Slocum shortly thereafter. When they woke in the morning, Goose was hungover, but not so badly that he couldn't get up and go with Slocum to the livery, to see to the horses.

There, they found the hostler Slocum had met the other day, and without thinking, Slocum asked him about the man Tim and Hobbins had seen do the shooting, then ride out of town. The hostler didn't recall the man, Slocum's description being as vague as the one given him, but he recognized the horse. Or thought he did.

"They say if it had any white on it?" he asked, toting a bale of hay.

"Said it was speckled on the rump," Slocum replied. "Other than that it was an Appaloosa."

"Well now, there was a feller rode in here the day before the shooting . . ." He heaved the bale over the corral fence, then reached through and cut the baling twine so that the bale fell open. "Rode an Appy colored like that. Chestnut, as I recollect. Only stayed one night. Came and paid for his keep the next afternoon, but he didn't ride out just then. Seen the horse tied up down a ways from the saloon, by the general store."

At this point Goose and Xander were both standing stock still, hanging on the stableman's every syllable.

Slocum said, "And you didn't recognize the feller?"

"Nope," said the hostler, coming back inside and peeling off his gloves. "Never seen him before. Kind of a nondescript kind of feller. Come to think of it, he kept turned away from me most all the time anyhow. You want them horses grained?"

Slocum nodded. "I owe you for yesterday, too. Grained all three of 'em."

"For the three, it'll be seventy-five cents a day if you want I should keep doing it."

"Yeah," said Slocum, without consulting Goose or Xander, and dug into his pocket for the cash. "Anybody else recognize him that you know of?"

The hostler shrugged. "All's I know is he walked on over to the hotel. They might be able to give you a name or somethin'."

"Thanks, I appreciate it," Slocum said, and went back to brushing Speck.

Goose attempted to detain the hostler further, but Slocum stopped him with a look. "Just wait," he said under his breath, smiling a little. "We don't wanna wear out the witness."

Hope had reignited in him—they might catch this son of a bitch yet!

After a hearty breakfast at the café, Slocum—this time with Goose and Xander—went back to the sheriff's office. Slocum was beginning to get the feeling that Sheriff Dodge didn't like him much, especially when the sheriff's greeting to him was a cranky "You again?"

Slocum bit his tongue and said, "We've come up with a little more evidence, Sheriff. Like to share it with you, if you've got a minute."

Goose was behind him, and Slocum heard him mutter, "You'd better, you bastard."

If Sheriff Dodge heard, he gave no sign. He just held out his hand toward the chairs on the opposite side of the desk. Slocum and Goose sat down. Xander leaned against the far wall.

"All right," said Dodge. "What is it this time?"

Slocum cut off Goose, who he felt was about to launch into the sort of conversation you should never have with a sheriff—at least, not while you were on his home turf—and began his tale.

He told Sheriff Dodge what the two fellows in the bar had told him about the horse and rider—and about the grumbled "Shit!" before the second shot.

He told about coming to the conclusion that the shootings had been accidental, a case of mistaken identity.

And then he told about what the hostler had revealed to him about the horse and his mysterious rider.

Sheriff Dodge sighed. "Which means you still got nothin'," he said, and started to stand, presumably to usher them out.

"No, I believe I got somethin'," Slocum insisted. "You aware of anybody who rides a chestnut Appy around here? Maybe somebody who don't come into town too often."

Again, he gave what little information he had about the rider's looks.

The sheriff just stared at him, then shook his head. "If he was here, he was a stranger to me and I sure as hell didn't see him. I'll ask my deputy when he comes in, but I ain't gonna promise you any better luck there."

Slocum stood up first. "All right. Just thought I'd check in with you first."

The sheriff seemed taken aback by the sideways compliment, and said surprisingly, "Feel free, anytime."

Harvey Smollets, having grown the beginnings of a beard over the time since he'd fled his ranch, was at the café, taking breakfast. Next, he planned to go to the general store and buy a pair of glasses—not for seeing, but to help disguise his face—and a bright green shirt, if one could be had.

He figured the green would be good luck, his mother having been from Ireland. He also planned to pick up a new pocketknife. He had been stopping, when it was convenient, at little towns along the way and gradually replacing the items in his wardrobe, and those in his possession, discarding the old ones in out-of-the-way places where they weren't likely to be found.

By the time he got farther north, he planned to be an entirely different person. Well, except for the accent. He'd tried before, but he could never seem to iron it out properly.

The waiter came by with the coffeepot, and he nearly said, "No, tea, please," out of habit. But instead he caught himself and held out his empty cup almost eagerly. Which was a good trick, because he couldn't stand the stuff.

To make up for it, he made sure to ask for sugar and cream, to help disguise the taste.

It was better, but it still wasn't Earl Grey.

He cut into his breakfast steak—well done, as usual—and thought of Slocum. He wished he knew what the man looked like. All he knew was that he was big and had dark hair, which is why he'd shot the wrong man—or so the Tucson deputies had informed him—that night out at Hiram Walker's ranch. Damn the man, anyway!

If he ever ran across him—even if it were fifty years from now—he'd give the son of a bitch what for, he'd vowed, and he was not a man to break his word. Slocum would die for ruining his life, and for cutting him off from his money, which now lay in the First Bank of Tucson, untouchable. All the cash he had was in his pockets, and it wasn't much.

He'd get Slocum, he vowed again, and cut off another bite of tough steak. "That bastard's mine!" he whispered before he jabbed the fork in his mouth.

Angrily, he began to chew.

"Where now?" Xander asked, once they'd left the sheriff's office behind. He could tell that his pa was as frustrated as all get out, but he understood—he thought, anyway—why Slocum wanted to keep the whole thing low-key. He just didn't think his pa got it.

Slocum said, "The general store, in case he stopped for provisions or ammunition. I ain't seen a gunsmith's shop, and I been keepin' my eyes peeled. Have either of you seen one?"

Goose shook his head, and Xander said, "No, sir."

Slocum grunted and headed down toward the general store. The others followed.

There, they found one Mr. Stanley, the owner and proprietor, who was sweeping out an otherwise empty store. After introductions were made, Stanley told them about a fellow who'd come in about that time, a fellow who'd tied his chestnut Appaloosa to the rail out front, bought some canned goods and ammunition, then left his horse out front.

"I figured he was goin' up to the saloon," Stanley said, resting an arm on his broom. He also gave a more complete description: shorter than any of the three questioners, dark hair, rugged features. The man had blue eyes, he thought. But he knew for sure that he had a scarred face: a knife scar, most likely, running from the corner of his mouth upward, to within a fraction of an inch of his eye.

"Right side?" Slocum asked.

"Yeah. How'd you know?" Stanley asked.

Slocum smiled. "Good guesser."

Goose, still looking a little awestruck at Slocum, muttered, "Well, thanks a lot for your time."

Xander, whose eyes had been on the candy jars since they set foot in the place, said, "Wait a second. Wanna buy some penny candy."

"Be right with you, boy." Stanley leaned his broom against a display of denim trousers and left them to go behind the counter.

While Xander pointed out what he wanted and Stanley got the scoop and started digging, Goose whispered, "Slocum? You know who the bastard is, don't you?"

Slocum nodded curtly. He whispered back, "Can't be nobody but Odie Ames. And that Appy he was ridin' used to be mine. Still is."

Kemo was a tall chestnut stallion, with a white blanket on his rump, who had slipped from an inattentive hostler's grasp the fall before. The horse was a little on the jugheaded side, but he reined good and could spin on a nickel and give you three cents change.

Goose blinked. "Who the hell is Odie Ames?"

"The stinkin' son of a bitch who shot your brother and nephew, and the very same bastard who stole my horse."

Miles to the south, Odie Ames was engaged in a high-stakes poker game, and he was losing. The fellow across from him had just raised, and the man next to him, on Odie's right, had seen the bet. Now it was Odie's turn, and he had exactly squat-nothing in his hand. He figured he could try to bluff, but he didn't feel much like it.

He put his cards on the table, facedown, and said, "Too rich for my blood, fellers." He picked up his whiskey and drained the glass, then pushed back from the table.

"Ain't you gonna stick around to see who takes the pot?" asked the man to his left, who had already folded.

Odie stood up. "Why?" he asked. "I know it ain't me."

The two still actively betting laughed. "Leave him be,

Ed," said the man across from his chair. He pushed four gold double eagles into the pot. "That's a hundred more to you, Ivan." Then he looked up at Odie again. "The man knows when he's beat."

"Or knows when he's just plain had enough, Swanson," grouched Ivan, before he cast down his cards and announced, "I fold, too. Lady Luck just ain't on my side, this afternoon."

Laughing, Swanson raked in the pot. "She ain't been on your side for as long as I've knowed you, Ivan."

They were still laughing as Odie left the saloon. He'd best stable his horse now, while it was still afternoon. He was lucky to have ended up with the Appy, he thought. Lucky that he looked enough like the horse's rightful owner that the hostler had handed him over, no questions asked. But he was unlucky, of late, in targeting marks. And that little incident up in Lonesome had just about taken the cake. Oh, there'd been occasions when he'd killed men he didn't have to. But he'd never mistaken a mark. Never, not once.

He had no idea who the hell he'd shot that night in Lonesome, but at least he'd kept his usual low profile. Nobody had seen him, he was fairly sure of it. And neither man had survived. Of this, he was certain.

When Odie Ames shot somebody, they stayed dead.

6

By the time Xander had his candy—six sacks' worth—and Goose had calmed down, they ventured up to the café and ordered their dinner. While they waited for their food, Slocum watched Xander, who made his way through those candy sacks like a gopher through a vegetable patch.

At one point, Xander caught him looking. He held out the bag. "Want some?" he asked. The bag held lemon drops.

Slocum shook his head and smiled. "Sorry, nope. How about you, Goose?"

Goose didn't even look at him. He just kept on staring at the wall, muttering, "Odie Ames. The slimy, cross-eyed son of a bitch," and breaking toothpicks.

He kept up this litany when their meal arrived, and clear through it until the dried apple pie made its appearance, by which time the mutter had lengthened to "That double-dealin', ham-fisted, tortoise-brained, *ugly* sonofabitching bastard!"

In part.

By the time they left the café, Slocum was ready to slug

him, just to shut him up for a while. He said, "Give it a rest for Chrissake, Goose?"

Oblivious, Goose said, "Give what a rest?"

Xander, who was digging for his candy again, said, "Pa, we know you don't like Odie Ames very much. You don't have to keep callin' him names."

Goose's face knotted. "Oh," he said, coloring with embarrassment. "Sorry, fellas. It's just that that lard-butted, horse-theivin', murderin', scrofulous—"

"Pa!" Xander cut in, and Goose finally apologized, and then fell silent.

"Let's go on over to Ezra's house," Slocum suggested. He knew if they went back to the hotel this early, Goose would start up again—and keep it up until long after bedtime.

Fortunately, both Xander and Goose agreed with him— Goose probably wanted to tell somebody new, and Xander likely went along out of self-defense.

And so they spent the evening lounging on Ezra's porch—and later, in his parlor—while Goose told Ezra about the murders (and murderer) at least six times, and Slocum and Xander picked through Xander's candy.

"Is he ever gonna get tired and drop it?" Xander, chewing a gumdrop, whispered to Slocum.

Slocum crunched down on a peppermint. "Only when Odie Ames is convicted. Or dead."

That evening, Harvey Smollets still had no idea he was in the same town with Slocum. He had passed Slocum, Goose, and Xander on the street without ever recognizing them. Although he could hardly be expected to. He'd never seen Slocum, and his only glimpse of the other two had been from across the road in Tucson, and through the second-story window of a lightless room.

And so he lived in a fool's paradise of sorts. But he hadn't forgotten. Not by a long shot.

After he had his dinner, he stopped in at the general store and bought a newish copy of *Wanted*, a pulp magazine in which wanted men were profiled, and which also contained a classified advertising section—most ads were placed by gunfighters or bounty hunters looking for work. It was the latter that Smollets wished to retain.

He figured that if he couldn't find Slocum, a professional would be able to.

Magazine in hand, he walked back to the hotel and settled in for an evening of combing the ads.

At about eight-thirty, Slocum and the Martins took their leave of Ezra Noonan, who had been theatrically yawning and stretching for the past half hour. Goose was still talking as they walked through the front door and out onto the porch.

"... an' he killed 'em, just killed 'em!" he finished as Ezra, smiling thinly and nodding, closed the door behind them. Slocum figured it'd be a good bit before they were invited back to Ezra's. Not that they'd been invited this time.

"Pa?" said Xander. "Pa, why don't you give it a rest. I mean, just for a while."

Goose turned angrily toward Xander, but Slocum spoke before he could. He said, "The boy's right, Goose. Just 'cause we got a strong theory don't mean we solved the case. Best to keep it quiet for a while, don't you think?"

Goose turned back to Slocum, opened his mouth, then snapped it closed again. He walked a few steps ahead, then turned back. "You fellers ain't any fun. It weren't your brother who got murdered. It weren't your nephew, either."

"What's fun have to do with any of that?" Xander asked.

Goose took off his hat and smacked it over his knee. "You know what I mean, goddamn it!"

Slocum intervened. He didn't want to be in on the beginnings of a family feud. He held up his hand. "Yeah,

Goose, we know what you mean. Just try and calm down. You know, take it down a notch or so. For the time being. I don't want you gettin' yourself all exhausted before we even get a line on where to find Odie." He almost added, *And my horse,* but thought better of it.

Goose slapped his hat back on his head, crossed his arms, and stared at the ground. At long last, he looked up. "I'm sorry, boys. It's just that . . ."

Slocum went to him and clasped his shoulder. "S'all right, buddy. I understand. We both do. It's a terrible tough thing."

"That's right, Pa," echoed Xander.

Goose rubbed roughly at his eyes. "Saloon or hotel?"

Slocum was hoping for the saloon, but he said, "Your choice."

"Fine," Goose said. "Then, the saloon."

The three of them made their way up the alley, then up the street to the saloon. They were out of good bourbon, Goose having drunk it all up the night before, but the place had pretty decent beer. And Goose didn't say a word about Odie Ames for the entire time they were inside, Slocum having warned him again while they were outside the bat-wing doors.

They ended up staying for a good hour before they made their way to the hotel and sleep.

All in all, it had been a good day for Slocum.

It had been a good day for Harvey Smollets, too. His copy of *Wanted* now boasted a red-circled classified ad for the services of one Odie Ames, with a post office box address in a town not thirty miles southeast of Lonesome.

Smiling, he read the ad again. Yes, it was the same Odie Ames, all right. The same one he'd hired over fifteen years ago, back in Denver, to take care of a little problem he was having with a certain city councilman. Ames had arrived, solved the problem with no muss or fuss, then left. Simple as that.

He was confident that Ames could take care of this little Slocum difficulty just as easily.

He began drafting a wire, which he planned to send as soon as the telegrapher's office opened in the morning.

Odie Ames had gotten a room in the hotel in Ashfork and settled in for the night, still trying to puzzle out a way to tell the parties that had hired him that he'd missed his mark back in Lonesome. It had never happened to him before, so he had no experience in giving clients bad news.

He supposed he'd have to give the money back. And that was the worst part, because he was counting on it to allow him a vacation. Not a long one, just long enough to let him rest up for a while. All this traveling got on a man's nerves.

He figured to head on home in the morning. It wasn't far. He could make it in a day. But this was one instance when shortness of distance wasn't a good thing. All the sooner that he'd have to tell Roman Gresh that his man had slipped through his fingers.

Roman Gresh wasn't a man you wanted to give bad news to. In fact, Roman wasn't even a man you'd want to talk to, period, unless you absolutely had to.

But Odie was going to have to.

Finally, he decided that in this case, his best bet was just to tell Roman the truth and hope for the best. That was, if there was any "best" where Roman was concerned.

At last, Odie fell asleep, but fitfully. He tossed and turned all night.

Slocum spent a restless night, too. He was concerned over his next step. Or more precisely, just what the hell his next step should be. Goose was asleep, thank God, on the bed across the room, snoring softly, and Xander was sprawled over his own bed, dead to the world. At least, Slocum thought, he finally had some privacy.

But he still couldn't sleep. At last, he got up, taking care that the rope bed didn't squeak, and grabbed his vest. He rolled himself a quirlie, then sat in the big armchair by the window. Staring down at the darkened street below, he lit it and took a long drag.

It was all he could do to keep from coughing and waking the room, not to mention the floor. He'd been smoking ready-mades for too long, he decided, once he'd finished nearly choking to death. They'd made him soft.

Back to business.

He supposed he and Goose and Xander could just keep hanging around Lonesome, but he had serious doubts that Odie would come back. Anybody with Odie's reputation surely wouldn't want to revisit the site of his latest failure. Maybe his only failure. Slocum didn't know.

It would help if he knew where Odie hung his hat, even temporarily. Then he'd at least have a starting point.

But all he had at this point was a name. This was a big country, and Odie could be anywhere in it.

He took another drag on his smoke, but this time not such an enthusiastic one, and was rewarded by a cough-free inhale. Better. Goose picked that moment to roll over, and the volume of his snores went up dramatically. Great, just great. If Slocum couldn't sleep before, this didn't bode well for future attempts at slumber.

He kept on staring out the window, hoping the answer as to finding Odie would come to him. But it didn't. By the time he fell back into bed, he'd made and smoked three quirlies, and managed to come up with exactly nothing. He was beginning to wish he'd never made that promise to Goose, beginning to wish that Goose had never crossed his path in the first place.

And, as always, to wish that instead of here, he was back

on Hiram Walker's spread, in the bed—and arms—of Samantha.

He finally fell asleep, and he dreamt of her charms—and her cooking—the whole night through.

7

Two days later, and Slocum was still in Lonesome, effectively trapped by Goose's inability to make up his mind.

Xander was ready to go, that was for certain. Slocum believed he'd agree to go anywhere, so long as it was some place besides Lonesome. Slocum had seen him eyeing one of the town floozies, and had also seen his rather clumsy advances rebuffed. Had the circumstances been different, Slocum would have stepped in and talked to the boy about it, but right at the moment, he figured getting Xander laid was the least of his worries.

Slocum was the one who needed to get laid, and bad.

However, things didn't look too promising on that front. He'd checked out the town's few soiled doves, and they were all a little *too* soiled for his taste. He was beginning to think that he'd have to skip town overnight to find himself a good, bad woman.

He had talked to the sheriff again, for what little good that was.

And he'd been out for a couple of long rides on Speck,

just to make sure he didn't get too used to hanging around in a stable all the time, getting fat.

But basically, Slocum was bored. Bored stiff. What he didn't know, however, was that that was about to change.

Like an answered prayer, Smollets's telegram had come into Odie Ames's hands that very morning. He didn't bother talking to Roman Gresh or even letting him know he was in town. He simply rode straight out, headed for Lonesome. It shouldn't take him more than a day to ride there and a day at most to do the deed. And maybe, while he was there, he could find his original targets. Then he wouldn't have to talk to Roman at all.

Everything was working out just fine. Sooner or later, it did, if you just let it run its course. That was his credo, anyhow.

All things were made right by the passage of time.

Slocum was sitting on a bench out front of the saloon when the stage pulled into the depot, catty-cornered across the street. He leaned back, leisurely rolled himself a quirlie, and prepared to watch the show.

He had no more than struck a lucifer when Xander slouched down on the other half of the bench. Slocum held the match to his smoke. "What you up to?" he asked the kid without looking at him.

The rustle of paper told him all he needed to know. Xander'd been to the general store again and got himself some more candy. Slocum swore that he'd never seen anybody as keen for sweets as that boy!

Xander held a paper sack under Slocum's nose. Slocum sniffed. Horehounds. He said, "No thanks," and went back to staring across the street. The team had already been unhitched and was being led down the street to the stable while the fresh team, already in the traces, was being harnessed into place.

As far as Slocum could tell, the coach had been emptied of passengers. Too bad they'd gotten out on the opposite side. It would have been something new to look at, anyway.

"Different kind?" asked Xander, beside him.

"What you got?" Slocum asked, more from boredom than anything else. Across the way, passengers were beginning to climb into the coach, and the driver was straightening out their bags up top.

He wished he could see better.

More paper rustled. "Got lemon drops and peppermint sticks, marshmallows, and suckers."

The driver called something down to a man standing on the other side of the coach, then nodded and turned around, sitting in his seat.

"What kind?"

"Lemon, orange, grape, and cherry, I guess." Xander held forth the sack. "Want one?"

The driver snapped his reins and hollered at his team. The off-lead horse half reared just as they pulled out, exposing the sidewalk and the people standing on it.

"Not now," muttered Slocum, who stood up as he spoke, brushing the luckless Xander aside. There, standing across the street, was about the prettiest little blond filly he'd seen in a month of Sundays. She'd just climbed off the stage, it appeared, since she reached down, picked up a carpetbag— which Slocum supposed could be nobody's but hers, judging by the surfeit of embroidered flowers on it, and the fact that all the other disembarked passengers were men—and started down the street, striding toward the hotel.

"Now that's more like it," Slocum muttered.

"What's more like it?" Xander asked. The girl was in her twenties, and to Xander, being only sixteen himself, Slocum imagined she must seem like an old lady.

"Where's your pa?" Slocum asked as he stepped past the boy and started to trail the woman down the sidewalk. Without being too obvious, of course.

"Ezra Noonan's."

"Go and check on him, all right? You hurry, and Ezra might ask you to stay for lunch."

"Sure!"

The kid disappeared like somebody had shot him out of a gun, and Slocum stepped up his own pace. The blond girl had just disappeared into the hotel.

"Miss Eliza Corning," she wrote in the register, then took her key and was up the stairs just as Slocum burst into the lobby.

The desk clerk looked up from his Sears and Roebuck catalogue and grinned. "Looker, weren't she?"

Slocum smiled. At least somebody else in this town had taste. He said, "Mind if I look at the register?"

"Be my guest." The clerk laughed as he spun the register around to Slocum. "Oh, I guess you already are, ain't you?"

Slocum laughed at the clerk's little joke, then bent down to peer at the book. "Miss Eliza Corning," it said. He was happiest to see the "Miss."

However, he was not so pleased when his eye caught the next name up. "H. Smollets, Esq."

He pointed at it and asked, "He still here?"

"Oh," said the clerk, surprised. "Thought you were lookin' for the lady."

"I was, but . . . he's an old acquaintance. What room's he in?"

The clerk checked. "Right down the hall from you. One-sixteen."

"And the lady?"

"One-twelve. You want I should tell Mr. Smollets you're here?"

"No, don't say a word. I'd rather surprise him, if you don't mind." Surprise wasn't exactly the first word that came to his mind, but it was good enough for the clerk.

"Whatever you say, sir. My lips are sealed." The clerk smiled.

"Thanks a lot," Slocum said as he turned and left the building.

"Hey! Ain't you gonna—" was the last Slocum heard from the clerk as the door shut behind him, and he began to walk as quick as he could, up toward the sheriff's office.

"What d'you mean, you can't do nothin'?" Slocum demanded.

Sheriff Dodge shrugged. "Ain't got no paper on him. 'Sides, that was over in Arizona."

"I thought murder was a capital offense," Slocum said, as calmly as he could under the circumstances.

"Ain't got no paper on him."

"Well, wire the sheriff in Tucson. He'll tell you. He shot my friend on his way out of town, too."

Again, Sheriff Dodge just shrugged his shoulders. "It probably ain't even the same feller. I swan, you run in here with every hangnail you get!"

Slocum simply turned and left, slamming the door behind him. He went directly to the telegrapher's office, where he sent a wire to Tucson and another to the federal marshal's office in Prescott. He ought to see some action out of somebody.

He wondered how the hell the town of Lonesome was still in existence if this was the caliber of lawman they normally voted into office.

Next, he hiked over to Ezra's house. He found Ezra, Goose, and Xander just sitting down to a lunch of roasted chicken. He declined the invitation to stay and eat, and instead said, "I need to talk to you in private, Goose."

Goose pushed back from the table and followed him up into the parlor. "What is it, Slocum?" he asked, eager to get back to the chicken.

He wasn't so eager when Slocum told him about Smollets being in town—and his being checked into the hotel right down the hall from them. Goose, whose shoulder was still giving him trouble, reacted out of all proportion.

In fact, he shouted, "That goddamn son of a bitch!" so loudly that Ezra and Xander came running from the kitchen.

"What? What?" shouted Ezra. "Is somebody hurt?"

Goose looked over, a snarl on his lips. "Not yet," he barked, "but somebody's gonna be!"

"Calm down, Goose!" Slocum shouted, and Goose did, after a moment. In fact, the whole room was subdued.

Slocum had to repeat to the others what he'd told Goose, and then added that he'd been to the sheriff's office, gotten no satisfaction, and then taken himself to the telegrapher's.

"That goddamn Sheriff Dodge has got no more business wearin' a badge than I got drivin' a train!" Goose railed. Although much more quietly than before.

"I would tend to agree," said Ezra, quietly. "When our former sheriff quit, Dodge was appointed by the city council. The chairman of which, I should add, is his brother-in-law."

"Figures," muttered Slocum.

Ezra put his hand on Goose's shoulder. "Let us hope, old friend, that the Arizona authorities take swifter action than we have locally."

"Amen to that," said Goose.

"Chicken?" asked Xander, and Goose was suddenly on his feet.

"Yeah," Goose said. "Let's eat."

Slocum pulled Ezra aside while the others walked back to the kitchen. "Keep him as calm as you can, all right?"

Ezra nodded wearily.

For Slocum, it was back to the café, then home to the hotel. Miss Eliza Corning didn't answer his knock on her door, so he went to bed.

Xander listened to his father and Ezra talk with gritted teeth. His pa was getting out of hand, and if Slocum had been there, he might have known what to do. But he wasn't, so Xander just sat there and listened.

His pa was talking about confronting Smollets, and rubbing his shoulder every few minutes. Hadn't he heard Slocum say that he'd alerted the Arizona authorities? Hadn't he heard that murder was a capital crime, and that they'd be in their authority to cross both territorial and state lines to apprehend Smollets?

He knew his pa was mad—who wouldn't be?—but facing off with Harvey Smollets was about the worst way to get revenge that Xander could think of. To his mind, Smollets was a deadly sniper. After all, he'd shot his pa—nearly killed him—from a perch eighty or ninety feet out, he guessed. And at night.

Of course, he understood that Smollets was looking for Slocum, and had thought that he'd killed him—but that didn't make him any less deadly. It just made him sloppy.

And as far as Xander was concerned, sloppy plus deadly was well past a lethal combination. If his pa went through with his plan, he could get a lot of people killed, himself included. Xander, if asked, would rather just leave Smollets to the authorities coming from Arizona, forget all about Odie Ames, and go back to Seattle with his pa and meet his family.

Again, he grabbed for one of the sacks in his pockets. He didn't much care which one it was, he just needed something in his mouth to take his mind off all this killing.

Apparently, Ezra agreed with him. Suddenly, he stopped Goose mid-threat and said, "Goose, my boy, you're much better off leaving this to the authorities." Goose made a face, and Ezra added, "The Arizona authorities. They'll be coming any day. Just you watch."

Xander's pa hung his head for a moment, then lifted it and said, "Don't trust 'em. Hell, I don't trust much of anybody, the way things have been goin' for me lately."

"Nonsense," Ezra said, then held his arm out toward

Xander. "Personally, I think you're one of the luckiest men it's my pleasure to know. Look at your fine son."

Xander stopped chewing his caramel and sat up a little straighter.

Goose looked at him, then back at Ezra. "That's true, Ezra," he said. "But I had to lose a brother and a nephew to get him. Don't seem fair somehow."

"Life ain't fair, Pa," Xander said quietly. "It just ain't."

If anyone knew about the the justice of life, or lack thereof, it was Xander. Born in a whorehouse, later stepfathered by a battering drunk, and raised in poverty, he'd had it worse than most. But then he'd found Slocum, who all his life he had been told was his father. He'd loved being Slocum's son. It was a dream come true to have been fathered by a real, honest-to-God, dime-novel hero. He couldn't have been prouder. And the fact that Slocum accepted him, once they finally met, was just the icing on the cake.

Later, when Slocum and Goose began comparing notes and Xander was foisted upon the redheaded Goose, he hadn't taken it badly, all things considered. He'd just made up his mind that some things didn't work out the way you wanted, and that was that.

Still, it was tough starting to call Goose his pa when he'd had Slocum as a father for about two weeks. Not that he didn't admire Goose. He did. Just not as much as the fabled Slocum, although he'd never admit as much to Goose.

He started chewing his caramel again, and slouched back into his chair to listen to Goose and Ezra argue some more. And eat a few more caramels.

8

Meanwhile, Odie Ames, having ridden the whole day through, stabled his horse at the livery. The hostler had gone home for the day hours before, and so Odie was on his own. He took note of the two other Appys stabled down the row and thought it odd that there should be three Appaloosas in the same livery at the same time. They weren't very common even in the Northwest, the home of the Palouse Indians, who raised them.

After stripping his horse of tack and tossing some grain in the bin and hay in the manger, he went to the hotel in search of this Smollets character. The name sounded familiar, and Smollets had wired that Ames had worked for him before. But not in Ames's living memory. Maybe it had been one of the myriad little jobs he'd taken years ago, just to keep body and soul together.

He was understandably curious.

He was also understandably nervous. Coming back to Lonesome so soon after that last foul-up hadn't been high on his list, but he needed the money. It was that simple.

The clerk was still on duty when Otis walked into the

lobby, and he sent Otis upstairs. He knocked on Smollets's
door, and it took Smollets a few minutes to get there. "Smollets?" Otis asked. He'd never seen the man before in his
life.

But Smollets responded with "Ames! Old friend! Come
in, come in! I would have recognized you anywhere!"

Smollets tried to pull him into the room, but Ames put
on the brakes. "I never seen you before in my life, mister."

Smollets let go of his arm. Sighing, he said, "Ten years
ago I was living in Denver. I wired you about a certain city
council member, and you—"

Ames suddenly came to life, and pushed Smollets inside, following him directly. He closed and latched the door
behind them.

"I remember," he said, arching a brow. "But you don't
look like you."

Smollets chuckled. "Thank you. I'm trying not to."

"Still got that English accent, though."

Smollets nodded. "May we talk about the mark now?"

Ames settled down in a comfortable armchair and put
his feet up on the footstool. "Go ahead. I'm listening."

Ames crossed in the hall with Goose and Xander, but they
didn't recognize him, not even when Xander, digging in a
sack for his last caramel, bumped into him. All Odie Ames
noticed about them was that they were both redheads and
looked like father and son. But his mind was on more important matters.

Slocum, for instance.

He hoped he hadn't let Smollets see through his veneer
of bravado. Being afraid of a mark was the last thing that
any gunfighter wanted to let on to, particularly to the man
who was hiring him—and getting him out of a sticky situation, to boot.

So he trudged down the stairs and checked into the hotel, noting by the register that Slocum himself had checked

in a few days ago. He wondered if Smollets knew. He hadn't mentioned it

Odie used the name Oscar Adams, one he hadn't used in years, but which at least let him keep his initials, and was assigned Room 101. He went back up the stairs, let himself into his room, and flopped on the bed.

This time, if he made it through it would be a miracle. He'd never met Slocum, only read some of the books and heard a lot of personal stories. And as filled with braggadocio as those books—and those personal stories—could be, and probably were, he still had a very bad feeling deep in his gut.

It was a long time before he got to sleep that night.

The next morning, Slocum and Goose were up with the sun, as usual, and taking an early breakfast at the café. Xander, who'd had a little too much candy for his own good the night before, only had eggs and toast, but Slocum and Goose made up for it by ordering a thick steak each, plus potatoes, biscuits, jelly, baked apples, and all the trimmings.

At least Goose was calmer today than he'd been last night. They were halfway through their breakfast before he mentioned Odie Ames, and when Slocum and Xander both ignored it, he didn't mention him again until after they'd paid for the meal and left the café.

"I keep tellin' you, Goose," Slocum argued, "we gotta get outta here and go lookin'. I can't think of a reason why he'd be crazy enough to come back to Lonesome, can you? Contrary to what you may be thinkin', I seriously doubt that anybody and everybody you ever wanted to get in your whole life is gonna just waltz into town and introduce himself."

"Look where?" Goose retorted. "You said yourself you ain't got no idea where to find him."

Slocum didn't answer him right away. They were coming up to the livery.

"See?" continued Goose. "Even you don't have a clue where to look. I say we just go shoot Smollets—that'd make me feel a little better, anyway—and then get outta town. Give it a month to find this Odie Ames. A month is all I'm askin', Slocum."

Slocum had stopped stock still in the open doorway of the livery, and Xander ran right into him.

"Oof! Sorry, Slocum," he said, picking himself up and brushing straw from his shirt. "Didn't even see you'd—"

Slocum completely ignored him. Staring straight ahead, he said, "Goose, I take it back. You're a man of genius."

There, in the stall across from him, stood another Appaloosa. It was Kemo, the horse that Odie Ames had "liberated" from Slocum almost a year ago.

The horse turned his head and his ears flicked forward when he spied Slocum. He whickered softly, and pawed the straw in his stall. Slocum moved forward and threw his arms around the horse's neck. "Hi, buddy, hi. How you been, huh?" Slowly, speaking softly, he went over the horse inch by inch, making certain there were no unattended wounds and that everything was in order. Everything was, with one exception.

"That son of a bitch," Slocum swore under his breath. "Odie Ames, you tinfoil bastard!"

Goose had wandered over. "Whassa matter?"

"That bastard, Odie Ames," Slocum snarled. "He's turned my stud horse into a gelding!"

Odie Ames, all-around bad guy and now a horse castrator, sat quietly in his hotel room, trying to work up the nerve to lift the latch and leave it. He knew what Slocum looked like, at least, as much as he could from the wanted posters and those book covers—which portrayed him as everything from a snarling villain to an angel of mercy—but Slocum didn't know him. At least, as far as he knew.

This gave him an edge.

But on the other hand, Slocum was braver and faster with a gun than he was.

Scratch the edge.

But Odie needed the money, and needed it in a hurry.

At last, avarice won out over fear. Slowly, he pushed himself up to a standing position and took the first step toward the door. And froze.

Get hold of yourself, Odie, he told himself. *This is no different from any other job.*

But he was lying to himself, and he knew it. Between what he had on Slocum and what Slocum had on him, he figured it was an even match, at best. And he had better get on with it.

But first, he had to check in with the hostler and make certain that he hadn't accepted his horse as a free gift, left by some generous stranger. He'd hate to leave go of the horse. He was a good one.

Odie took a deep breath and started forward, toward the door. Three more steps and he was there with his hand on the latch. Then outside in the hallway. He checked both ways—it was vacant. Good.

Heart still pounding in his chest, he started down the steps.

Still annoyed, Slocum and the Martins had adjourned to the other end of the livery to grain and groom their horses. Goose's Kip had somehow managed to smear his left flank with mud, and Goose was angrily attempting to curry it off.

"You ain't gonna get that with just a curry, Pa," Xander offered. "Best take him outside to the water trough."

Slocum agreed, but was still too angry to say anything. Goose apparently did, too, and quickly slipped a rope through Kip's halter, then led him from his stall to the outside. He began the tedious process of dipping water from the trough and washing down Kip's left flank.

"You were right," Slocum finally said to Xander. "Good call. For a minute there, I thought Goose was just gonna shoot him."

Xander laughed. "No way. He was tellin' me the other night how he's had Kip since he was a baby. Bottle-raised him and everything." When Slocum raised a brow, Xander added, "Kip's mama got killed by a mountain lion."

Slocum nodded. "Most fellas would'a shot the foal. Figured it'd be too much trouble."

"Not my pa," Xander said proudly, then hesitated a second before he added, "I don't think you would'a, either. You're both a couple'a softies when it comes to horses."

"Oh," said Slocum, watching the boy carefully and gently clean his gelding's ears. "And you're one to talk?"

Xander grinned. "Eagle's special. He takes good care'a me, and I take good care'a him."

"Partners?" Slocum asked.

Xander seemed to think a moment, then nodded his head. "Exactly. Partners." He rubbed Eagle's forehead, and the horse closed his eyes and leaned into him.

Slocum nodded. "The way it oughta be. Most fellas treat their horses like they was some kind'a machine instead of a livin', breathin' creature. Horses can hurt, horses can pine, horses can hold grudges, just like folks can." He paused. "Wish that hostler'd show up. I wanna ask him what happened to the feller that dropped off Kemo."

"Funny name for a horse," Xander mused. "What's it mean?"

"I used to know a feller down around Phoenix, name of Jack Swilling. He had this Indian friend, always hangin' around him and doing his errands. Anyhow, the Indian called Swilling 'Kemosabe.' Not sure how you spell it, but I took it to mean 'friend,' or at least somethin' close. And horses can't spell worth beans, anyhow."

Xander laughed. "I'll have to remember that one!" They heard footsteps from outside. "Must be the stableman comin' now," said Xander.

But it wasn't the stableman.

It was Odie Ames.

9

Miss Eliza Corning checked her makeup and hat for the final time, picked up her purse, and let herself out of her room, locking it behind her. Once downstairs, she asked the clerk where she might find some breakfast.

"Next door, ma'am," he stammered, a little tongue-tied. But he added, "It's a good'un."

She flicked him a smile, a smile that made his day, if not his week. He was beginning to look a little sickly, so she took her leave and headed for the café.

Men were so silly. They always reacted to her in that manner, all quivery and careful with their words. In a way, it was nice. She rather liked it, having power over men. But what she'd really like was a man who'd stand up to her, or at least meet her on an equal footing.

Once inside the café, it was the same thing. The waiter fawned, the other customers—all male, with the exception of what looked like a farm wife—stared, then looked away when she turned her head their way. Same old same old.

She ordered toast, bacon, and eggs, over easy, and black coffee, and was not surprised when it came so quickly while the other customers waited. She was always served promptly, no matter how long the line was in front of her. Normally, she would make a comment or complaint to the waiter, but this morning she was so hungry that she forgot all about it.

And the food was excellent.

She had taken no more than three bites of her toast when the café door opened and a new face walked in. He was dark, a little better than medium height, and walked in as if he owned the place. He was rugged-looking, but not in a handsome way. More in a dangerous way, she decided. There was something behind those eyes . . .

"Good morning, my dear," he said as he stopped by her table.

"Good morning, sir. I don't believe we've been introduced," she said, in the coldest manner possible. She was actually taken with the English accent, just not with the man behind it.

The stranger bowed slightly and doffed his hat. "Please pardon me. I am Harvey Smollets, Esquire. And you would be?"

"A lady trying to eat her breakfast in peace, Mr. Smollets."

She heard a snicker escape the farm wife's lips, and knew that she had at least one ally.

"I see," he went on. "Then I shall leave you to finish it."

Thank God, she thought as he turned toward another table and pulled out a chair. Facing her, of course. Some men seemed incapable of taking *no* for an answer. At least, all the way to the core.

She was just lifting her first bite of egg to her lips when two shots, very close together, rang out nearby. She leapt to her feet, along with most of the other patrons, then stood there, wondering what to do next. Some of the men had gone to look out the window, and although she didn't follow them, she heard one say something about the livery across the way.

Surely they didn't shoot horses in town! Barbaric practice, anyway. Horses were such majestic creatures.

She sat back down in her chair, collected herself, and finally took a bite of her eggs. Delicious!

And then, out of the corner of her eye, she saw Mr. Smollets. It was not the most appetizing sight, for he had a large grin plastered over his face, which was turned toward the front window. How anyone could be pleased at the death of a horse was beyond her ken!

Before she realized it, she snapped, "How dare you, sir!"

He turned toward her and touched his hat's brim. "Pardon me, madam," he said, the unwholesome smile still plastering his face. "Pardon me all to hell."

"Stay back!" Slocum demanded, and Xander—confused and flustered and scared nearly to death—obeyed.

"What happened?" asked Goose, still outside with Kip. He was a little shaky, too, and he was staring at the body. It lay about ten feet from him, midway between himself and Slocum. It was a man, and he appeared to be very dead.

Slocum walked over to him, his gun still out of its holster and at the ready, and kicked him in the side. Deadweight. He kicked the pistol from the man's hand, then slowly holstered his own gun.

"What the hell happened?!" Goose demanded again.

"Goose," Slocum said, bending to the body, then rolling it over, "meet the son of a bitch who killed your brother and your nephew." He stared down for a moment, then flicked his gaze toward Speck, who was dancing nervously in his stall. "And who also stole one horse from me and goddamn shot another," he added, going to the horse.

He saw where Ames's slug had wounded Speck, creasing his butt but leaving no metal behind. Lucky shot. It could have been much worse.

Xander just stood there, eyes wide, hanging on to Eagle's halter and mouthing, "Jesus!" over and over again.

"What the hell's goin' on out here?!" Sheriff Dodge shouted from across the street. He came toward them at a brisk walk, with a nasty expression twisting his lips. "Who the hell's firin' their pistol in my town in the middle of the—" He stepped into the shadows of the livery and was immediately hushed. He stood stock-still, staring down at Ames's body.

Several minutes passed before he spoke again. "W-who is he?"

Slocum, who was swabbing Speck's wound with his bandana, spoke. "Odie Ames. Gun for hire. Was, anyway. Killed Goose's brother and nephew, and stole my horse, Kemo, about a year back. Somebody—probably Smollets— must'a sent him after me, 'cause he just walked in and drew. No warnin' or nothin'."

"I heard two shots," said the sheriff.

"Mine's in his chest," Slocum said, pointing. "And his shot very nearly ruined a real good saddle pony." He held up the bloody rag, displaying the smear of blood on Speck's blanket.

"If he just walked in and drew, how is it that you got your gun out first?" Sheriff Dodge demanded.

"Guess I'm faster than he was," Slocum said, and wiped at Speck's rump again.

"That's the honest truth," volunteered Goose. "I never seen nothin' like it! All happened in the space of a breath— no, half a breath!"

Xander slowly nodded, backing up his father's words. The look of awe still hadn't left the boy's face.

"I don't know about this . . ." the sheriff began, then trailed off.

It seemed to Slocum that the sheriff didn't seem to know about much of anything, but he kept his mouth shut. He knew better than to play mind games with appointed officials, particularly those who were related to their appointers. They tended to be a little . . . mulish. All right, they tended to be pigheaded, and made up the rules as they went along. Sheriff Dodge didn't seem to be any exception to the general rule.

Slocum said, "Those are the facts, Sheriff. I don't know why he'd be stupid enough to come back into Lonesome after killin' those other two men so recently, unless somebody hired him to get me. Which seems sort'a reasonable, considerin'."

The sheriff didn't answer him, just stared. Then then he spoke. "Considerin' what?"

"Considerin' that Harvey Smollets is in town," Slocum said, after a deep breath. "Although not for long, I hope. Yesterday, I wired the Tucson marshal, and also the territorial folks up in Prescott. Don't imagine it'll take 'em too long to get here."

"You know, the folks I have the hardest time with are them that should be in jail themselves," Dodge snarled. "And that means you."

"I ain't been charged with anything that stuck," Slocum replied evenly. "Not once."

"'Cause you got a talent for unstickin' yourself."

Slocum nodded. "It's easy when you ain't done nothin' wrong."

From the shadows came Xander's voice. "Slocum's one of the good guys, Sheriff. I seen him bust up a gang of rustlers. Smollets's gang, as a matter of fact."

Sheriff Dodge ignored him and kept his eyes riveted on Slocum. Slocum figured that if Dodge could have growled like a bulldog, he would have been the recipient.

"Here comes the undertaker, I think," Goose boomed from outside. "Sam Neil."

Sure enough, a thin figure—dressed in black, right up to his stovepipe hat and down to his dress shoes—stepped into the livery. "Morning, Sheriff Dodge," he said. "Gentlemen."

With a quick glance he took in the body lying on the stable floor, then returned his attention to the sheriff. "Are my services required?"

Dodge let out a deep breath, then said, "Yeah. Lemme go through his pockets first, then he's all yours."

"Excellent, excellent," muttered the undertaker, pulling a small pad of paper and a pencil from his breast pocket. "Name?"

"Odie Ames," said Slocum, and before the undertaker could ask, he spelled it out for him. "And no," he added, "I don't know whether Odie's short for anythin' or not."

Across the street, at the café, a small crowd had gathered both inside and out, each person speculating on the goings-on at the livery.

"Reckon somebody's got shot," said one tall wag. "Sam Neil's over there. You hear one shot or two?"

"You mean you reckon somebody's dead, then," remarked his companion. "Undertakers only show up for folks who ain't gonna get home by their own power. And two shots, real close together."

Another man offered, "Could be that Neil just heard the shots an' went over lookin' fer work. You now how fellers in his line are. Could be he didn't find none."

"Naw, he'd be outta there by now."

"Mayhap he's just hangin' around, hopin' for the best."

The men in the crowd laughed.

All except for Harvey Smollets, that was. He had left the café (and left the pretty blonde behind) and come outside, only to be caught up in the wild speculations in the banter of the crowd. He'd best be well away before anyone came out.

"You remember that time when Roland Whitiker got himself plugged in the head by the out-of-towner down by the saloon? Hell, Sam Neil was the first one there, savin' for ol' Roland and whoever it was shot him!"

Smollets turned on his heel and headed for the hotel, reminding himself to oil his hair when he got back. Arizona was too blasted hot for hair oil, but northern California was just right, especially now that it was heading toward fall.

Besides, it would further help to hide his identity.

And then again, he couldn't be entirely certain who would come walking out of the livery—Ames or Slocum. If Slocum came walking out under his own power, he wanted to be hidden away in his hotel room where he could break something. Maybe several somethings.

And have some quiet to make a new plan.

And if Odie walked out in the same condition, he wanted to be someplace where he could whoop up a storm without drawing attention to himself.

He hurried back to the hotel, and up to the second landing. He could watch the livery from the landing window.

10

Not too many minutes later, the folks watching the livery door saw the sheriff back out, carrying Odie Ames's shoulders. And a moment later, Xander followed, Odie's booted feet in hand. They were having a little trouble with the body, so Goose put down his bucket and went to help Xander. The undertaker led the way, and they followed him down the street to his parlor.

Slocum stayed behind, still wiping off Speck's wound, then applying some unguent to the area. The slug had cut a shallow groove about three inches long across the gelding's croup. If it had been a fraction of an inch lower, Slocum would have been trying to dig it out instead of cleaning the site of its passage.

When he was finished with Speck, he went to Kemo. He could already tell that the horse hadn't been missing any meals—in fact, he would have liked him a tad leaner—and an inspection of his mouth, lips, and teeth showed no bridle abuse either. Although he wasn't too happy to find some freshly healed scars on the gelding's flanks—spur marks. He growled to himself. If ever a horse hadn't needed to be

71

shown a spur, it was Kemo. He'd always been ready to go, and all Slocum had ever had to do to get top speed out of the Appy was to lean forward a little and give him a free rein.

Pissed off about the scars on his newly reclaimed Appy's sides, Slocum started to curry him down, and was amazed at the dust cloud that rose up around the horse. He obviously hadn't had a really good curry for a long time, and Slocum could tell that Kemo was appreciating this one by the groans that came from the animal.

He kept up the currying, flicking the dirt off the horse with a body brush held in his left hand, and by the time he had finished, he reckoned that he'd taken about ten or twelve pounds of hair and dirt off the animal. And there was more left to come out.

But Slocum decided to leave it for another day—and maybe for a bath, to help loosen up what was left—and moved on to Xander's Eagle, who was waiting patiently at the back of the barn, half-groomed.

He gave Eagle a quick but thorough currying, slicked him down with the body brush, then put him back in his box stall. By the time he'd done the same with Kip, the hostler showed up. "Finally," breathed Slocum.

"Mornin'," said the hostler lazily, holding up a hand.

"Mornin' yourself," replied Slocum. "You missed a lot of stuff goin' on."

"Oh, I doubt that," the hostler said. "Nothin' much ever happens round here."

When Slocum told him what had transpired, however, the hostler had to lean hard against a stall door, the color drained from his face.

"Are you kiddin' me?!" he said, once he regained the ability to form words.

"I don't kid," answered Slocum. "Ask the sheriff or the undertaker it you don't believe me. Hell, you can ask half the town. Seems like they were all out on the street." He shoved Kip out of the way and latched his stall door. "By the way, is that last box stall rented out?"

The hostler shook his head dumbly. "Fine," said Slocum, unlatching Kemo's lead rope. "I wanna move him down there."

Slocum was halfway down the aisle before the hostler thought to say, "You payin' for this? And when'd he come in?"

"Must'a come in the night, sometime. The fella that got killed rode him in, but he stole him from me 'bout a year back."

The hostler named his price and Slocum paid not only for Kemo, but paid the other three horses up to date as well. He figured the sheriff sure wouldn't be on his side when he claimed Kemo, and it wouldn't hurt to have some backup from the stableman. *Let's just keep everybody happy,* he thought to himself.

About that time, he heard Xander and Goose coming down the street. By the time he'd turned Kemo out into his roomy new stall, they had entered the barn.

"Get Odie delivered?" he asked, while behind him Kemo pulled his usual box stall act—he dropped down to his knees, then his side, then rolled.

"What the hell's that crazy horse doin'?" asked Goose.

"What's it look like?" replied Slocum as Kemo wriggled back and forth in obvious ecstasy, scratching his back. "What about Odie?" he asked again.

"Got him delivered," said Xander. "Went through his pockets, too."

"He had a little book on him," Goose added. "Must'a used it for writin' down assignments. Last one was for Lonesome and the target was you."

Xander said, "Tell him the important part!"

"Yeah, yeah," said Goose. "The man that hired him was Harvey Smollets, and he was supposed to meet him at the hotel."

"You tell the sheriff?" Slocum asked.

Goose nodded. "He's the one what found it."

"He doin' anythin' about it?"

Goose shook his head. "Not that I know of."

Xander snorted. "Aw, he's an old goof. You an' I both know he ain't gonna do nothin', either. The coward. And the book even said he'd been here before, when Uncle Bill and Badger were here!"

"Mention 'em by name?" Slocum asked. Behind him, Kemo climbed to his feet and shook himself off like a giant dog. The straw flew every which way.

Goose shook his head. "Nope. The names in the book were Bob and Ted Cross."

"Sheriff ever heard of 'em?" asked Slocum. He certainly hadn't.

"Didn't say," said Goose. "Didn't give no sign, neither."

But the stableman had something to say. He reached for his back pocket and pulled out a pad of paper, then turned the pages backward. "They was here," he said. "Thought I recognized the names. They rode in on the fourteenth and rode out . . . the same day I got the Martins ridin' in."

"But we didn't—" Xander cut in.

"He means your Uncle Bill and your cousin Badger," Slocum said, in a tone that said, *Hush up*.

Xander colored and muttered, "Oh . . ."

After witnessing the debacle at the livery—or at least, what he could see of it from the hotel landing's window—Smollets had taken immediate action: he'd dashed to his room, thrown his few possessions in his carpetbag, paid his bill, then set off to the stable.

When he peeked around the corner and saw men inside, talking, he'd backed off immediately and hugged the outside of the building, in a place where he could easily see them coming, but where he wouldn't be noticed unless they were looking for him.

And they weren't. At least, they weren't looking where he was sitting. They were hotfooting it, all three of them, across the street, toward the hotel. Probably with him on their minds.

Although he now knew which one was Slocum. Odie Ames had been some help, at least. God rest his soul, Smollets thought belatedly, and crossed himself.

He waited until the three disappeared into the lobby, then hurried into the stable. "My horse!" he called to the hostler. "Now!"

"Gone?" Slocum said, repeating the desk clerk's word. "When did the son of a bitch leave?"

"Not long ago," said the clerk. "Came barrelin' down those stairs like—well, like I told you. Threw me three dollars for last night—and a tip, I guess—and then he was gone. Last I seen of him. Sorry." He shrugged.

The desk clerk couldn't have been over twenty. Even if he'd had a rope and tried to hog-tie Smollets, he probably would have ended up dangling from the chandelier, head-first.

"Xander," Slocum said, turning. But he spoke to nothing but air. The boy had left the door swinging behind him, and Slocum could just see flashes, through the swinging door, of him running back across the street, to the livery.

"Aw, Jesus," he muttered, then said, "C'mon, Goose, we've gotta catch him!"

Both men raced for the door, and were caught, jammed up, trying to make it through at the same time. Slocum finally managed to turn to one side and holler, "Go!"

As he felt Goose slip past him, he turned to race after, only to find a young blond girl blocking his path. Her arms were crossed and she looked annoyed. She opened her mouth to say something—probably cutting—but before she could, he put his hands on her shoulders and lifted her to one side.

"Pardon me all to hell, ma'am," he said, and ran for the stable.

He didn't realize until he was nearly there that she was the little blonde he'd seen get off yesterday afternoon's stage.

Smollets was gone. Even Xander, the first one to come plowing into the livery, had missed him by over a minute, and of course the hostler hadn't seen in which direction he'd galloped off.

Slocum was fit to be tied! He asked for a complete description of the horse, of the tack, and of the rider, as he presently looked. And he asked the hostler to repeat every word Smollets had said, hoping there'd be a clue in there somewhere.

But there wasn't.

So he sent Xander and Goose off in different directions and he went in a third, asking people on the street if they'd seen a man riding a horse of the hostler's description barreling out of town.

And no one had. Which only left one direction—north.

Slocum, Goose, and Xander spent the night in the open countryside. Slocum had managed to pick up Smollets's trail, mostly by default. His was the only set that galloped for so far, as if he were afraid the devil himself were on his trail.

And he's right, thought Slocum as he waited for the coffee to boil. Xander had shot them a couple of nice quail, and Slocum had fixed a stew, which was just beginning to bubble in its pot. He was glad they'd stopped at the general store for provisions on the way out of town.

Goose hadn't wanted to. He'd wanted to ride Smollets down as soon as possible and do all manner of colorful—and mostly impossible—things to him. Goose tended to be a whole lot of talk and not so much action—although he was a good man to have around during a gunfight. Slocum had taken to riding a good bit ahead just to escape the noise.

If he heard the expression "I'll have his guts for garters!" one more time, he thought he might be physically ill.

The coffee was ready, and Slocum poured out three cups, remembering to dose Xander's with several spoons of sugar.

"Thanks!" Xander said, accepting it happily.

Goose took his with a nod, but that was all. Thank God. He had taken it upon himself to stop up his own dam, at least during their dinner. And Slocum hoped he'd keep it that way all night.

Slocum handed Xander the plates and forks, and let him dish up the stew. He'd bought a loaf of sourdough bread in town, too, and he ripped off a hunk, then passed the loaf to Goose. Goose grunted, pulled off a piece, and handed it to Xander.

And so they spent the night in silence.

11

By five o'clock, Harvey Smollets was already up and on his way. He had spotted the pinpoint glow of Slocum's small fire last night, panicked, and moved his camp on through the dark another mile or two. He still didn't feel safe enough, however, to fitfully sleep past four.

Slocum didn't even wake until six, and had to rouse Goose and Xander out of their bedrolls, among other things, before they got on their way.

They easily found the site of Smollets's first camp, and his second. And they moved out along his trail as surely as day follows night.

They were quiet today, too, for which Slocum was eternally grateful. He didn't know if Goose had lost his voice or simply run out of nasty things to say about Smollets, but he didn't press him. He was afraid that if he got Goose wound up, he might not wind down until sometime next week.

Xander took his clue from Slocum, and didn't say a word, either.

Slocum rode Kemo today and led Speck. To be honest, he couldn't decide which he wanted to keep. Kemo was an old friend, and still as sensitive to the bridle as ever. But Ames having him gelded had altered his personality, if horses could be said to have them—and Slocum thought so. True, it had eliminated some of his more irritating qualities, but it seemed to have dulled other, more endearing traits.

For instance, he no longer did those abrupt about-faces when he sensed other horses coming up behind him: a practice that other riders might have found annoying, but that Slocum got a kick out of. It only took him by surprise once. After that, he paid attention to Kemo's ears. They flicked once, and in a different sort of way, just before he turned.

But he didn't turn anymore. Neither did he nicker and call to any horse coming up on them from any direction, or do any manner of other little things that used to be his habits. Slocum felt as if somebody still had possession of half of his horse. But having half was better than having none of him.

Still, by the time they stopped for the noon meal, he was pretty damn sure that Kemo was the horse he'd sell. If only Ames hadn't been so goddamn quick with the gelding knife!

Little did they realize it, but they were within one hour of catching up with Smollets, who had holed up in a rock outcrop in order to grab some quick lunch and rest his horse. "His horse" had no name besides "my horse" or "Smollet's horse" or just plain "*horse*." He didn't believe in naming animals, in personalizing them. They were just animals, after all.

Although he had to admit he would have liked someone or something, right now, that he could talk to, something that had a name.

But he'd be damned if it'd be a stupid horse.

Meanwhile Tucson's sheriff and the federal marshal's office up in Prescott had sorted things through, and the sheriff had agreed to turn the matter over to the marshal's office.

Deputy Marshal Clint Grover had been dispatched first thing the day before yesterday, and had already crossed the California border. He had a few mountains left to ride across, but he figured to make it to Lonesome tonight.

He'd been sent because he knew Slocum. Of course, a lot of the deputies knew him on sight or well enough to say hello to, but Grover had actually worked with him on a case in the not-too-distant past, and spoke highly of him, as did the correspondence the U.S. Marshal's Office had received from Tucson.

The correspondence did not speak so highly of one Harvey Smollets, the escaped murderer and cattle thief, who was the target of this little trip to California. It was Grover's job to round him up, take him into custody, and haul him back to Arizona for trial. Although he supposed he could just shoot him, he thought, grinning. After all, Smollets was wanted for not one, but two murders, plus an attempted murder, all other charges aside.

He was a bad one.

The climb was too steep for his horse, who was already tired, so he slipped off and began to lead the gelding uphill. That didn't work too well, either, although the game trail they were following showed plenty of deer tracks. They finally came to a place that was nearly level, and he straightened the horse out, crossways on the path, so that he might rest for a while. Then he slumped to the ground opposite him.

"They didn't put this on the enlistment form, did they, Dusty?" Grover said, a smile twitching at the corners of his mouth. "Sign-up sheet. Whatever they called it."

Dusty, a round-muscled buckskin, nosed the scant brush along the path, looking for something edible. He found a few blades of grass and began to chew.

"You ain't the only one who's hungry," Grover growled, "but I'm waitin' till we get clear of these trees and on the downhill side of the slope. Slope! Now that's a good one!"

He laughed and looked up the trail. It seemed to go straight up forever. He wished he could harness up some of those damned deer and let them haul him and Dusty over the crest!

By galloping a good bit of the way, Smollets was now a good hour and a half ahead of Slocum. His horse hadn't appreciated it, though. Right now, it was walking slowly, head down and dripping sweat, the lather falling from its neck and croup in handfuls.

Smollets wasn't concerned, though. He'd run the horse like this yesterday, and it hadn't hurt it any. Over the long term, anyhow.

He couldn't be that far from Sacramento, he thought hopefully. It would be easy to get lost in Sacramento, even easier in San Francisco.

That was his hope. To make it to San Francisco and get himself involved in silver mining. He'd never been a silver magnate before, and he thought it was about time. Of course, he could have been involved in mining back in Arizona, too, but the cattle venture had just dropped into his lap, and he'd taken advantage of it.

Thank God he hadn't got involved in mining! Just think of how many thousands more he would have had to leave behind!

The horse stumbled, nearly throwing Smollets from the saddle, and he quirted it across the shoulders as hard as he could. It did nothing but keep walking, though. Lazy beast.

Eight steps later and Smollets felt the horse about to do something else. Lay down, for instance.

"No, no, you lazy bastard!" he shouted as he slithered off the horse's side and landed on the ground. On his feet, thankfully.

The horse seemed to regain itself, but then its knees buckled and it went down with a low, agonized groan.

"Filthy thing! Filthy son of a hog-swine!" Smollets

railed, lashing out again with his crop. This time he caught the gelding just behind the near elbow, but the lashing did no good. Other than an involuntary twitch, the horse gave no sign that he'd even felt it.

Smollets kept whipping the horse for quite some time, his anger growing with each blow, until his arm finally gave out and he collapsed to the ground in a slump.

The horse was dead.

Slocum followed the galloping hoofprints of Smollets's horse through the scrubby desert at a slow lope, so as not to lose them. Goose had had a turn at leading, but had gone too fast and lost the trail. Now that they had it again, Slocum was in no way going to lose it.

He signaled for a slowdown, and Goose, who'd been following about two horse lengths back, was at his side in no time. "What's wrong!" he demanded. "Why are we slowing down?"

"For the horses," Slocum said, in what was close to a snap. "I know you're in a big hurry to catch Smollets, but I'm not gonna run our horses into the ground like he's doin' with his."

Goose had no answer to this, but Xander, who had caught up to them during Slocum's tirade, agreed. "Looks to me like his horse's strides are gettin' shorter and shorter. An' I passed up a fresh-thrown shoe back there, 'bout a quarter mile ago." He pointed with a jabbed thumb back the way they'd come.

Slocum nodded. "Yeah, the tracks show it. Our man Smollets is ridin' a dead horse, whether he knows it or not." He growled part of the last sentence. "Wouldn't be surprised to find him over the next hill. Which means I want you boys to fan out and have your rifles ready, just in case. All right?"

Xander nodded and Goose said, "Right." A grin was already replacing his frown.

"Don't ride clear to the crest until I give the signal," Slocum added. "We'll make easy targets if he's down there."

"Check," said Goose.

"Right," said Xander.

The three men rode forward, Xander going to the left and Goose going to the right.

U.S. Deputy Marshal Clint Grover—and Dusty—had finally made it over the mountain, and were now worming their way down the opposite side, toward the low hills beyond. To tell the truth, Grover wasn't exactly certain where he was going to come out—north or south of Lonesome. He'd never made this trip before, and he wasn't sure which mountain it was that he and Dusty had just climbed, only that it was—finally—the last in a long series.

At last, they reached the foothills, and Dusty seemed as relieved as Grover to finally find the traveling a bit easier. The vegetation was thinning out, too, with the trees—mostly towering pines—behind them and only cedars and low growth ahead. Grover imagined that eventually, he'd ride right out onto scrub desert.

He'd never seen an ocean, so he hoped his travels would take him near it. Rather, that Smollets's travels would. He wouldn't know until he found Slocum.

When he'd ridden with Slocum before, he found him completely to the contrary of the man painted by the books and the legend. Oh, he was fast with a gun, all right, and tough as nails, and Grover guessed that if the man stripped down to the skin, you'd find the scars left by a thousand bullets, knives, lances, and arrows. The man was a magnet for implements of destruction, although none of them seemed to work on him.

They'd followed a scrawny, axe-faced killer by the name of Lute Farrow down through New Mexico. And although Slocum seemed to be madder about Lute having stolen his

Appaloosa than about the murder of a Catholic priest, he was more than willing to help drag him back to the courts for punishment. On foot, though. Slocum led his reclaimed horse all the way up to Prescott, with Lute tied to his tail, shank's mare.

That Appy had been a nice pony, all right, but you wouldn't find Grover riding one. Too loud for his taste, and this one had been the loudest kind—spotted all over like a leopard.

Grover crested the first hill, stopped, and pulled out his binoculars. With any luck, he could see a town from here. He scanned the distance and had no luck finding even a chimney, but far off, almost too far for him to make out, what looked like a man was pointing what looked like a rifle at a distant ridge to the south.

And it seemed that the man had barricaded himself behind a downed horse.

12

A little before they topped the ridge, Slocum signaled both Xander and Goose to dismount, then followed his own instructions. Rifle in hand, he got down on his belly and crawled to the top of the ridge.

He'd been right. Smollets was down below, hunkered behind his horse's carcass. The horse was covered in blood. Smollets must have whipped him to death when he couldn't go on.

Slocum felt his blood begin to boil. If Smollets had known what the hell he was doing, that horse could have lasted him years and years. And now he'd died for Smollets, died for a homicidal son of a bitch who didn't give a shit about him or anybody or anything else.

It just figured, didn't it?

Slocum kept his head low and sited his long gun on Smollets's head, which kept bobbing down below the horse's rib cage and out of sight.

Slocum took a deep breath, more to get control of himself than anything else, and then, Smollets's head having disappeared once again, he sited the place where it had been before. His target was a long way off—nearly four hundred yards, to the best of his reckoning—but Slocum was sure he could hit the murdering son of a bitch.

At least, if there was a God upstairs in heaven, he could.

He flicked his eyes skyward, then quietly sited his rifle once more.

U.S. Deputy Marshal Clint Grover topped the next foothill and once again pulled out his binoculars. Yes, that shape was indeed a man pointing a rifle, and he was hiding behind what looked like a dead horse.

Grover swung the binoculars to the south, to the top of the ridge there, and saw three tiny specks of color, each one connected to what looked like a rifle's barrel.

Just what the hell was going on down there, anyway?

Well, whatever the heck it was, it wasn't going to go any further until somebody explained themselves to the authorities. Meaning him.

Although he doubted they could hear it, because of the distance and the terrain, he yanked his rifle from its boot, aimed it up in the air, and fired a shot.

He peered through the binoculars again and waited a moment.

Yes! They'd heard it. The one crouched behind the horse turned on his side, aiming his rifle toward Grover's hills. And the ones on the ridge lowered their rifles. Or hell, they could have been holding up brickbats, for all he could tell at this distance!

He jammed his rifle back into its boot, and urged Dusty to start his skitter down the far side of the hill.

Slocum looked toward the eastern hills, where the shot had originated. It was hard to tell exactly where it had come from, and he could only guess at a general area. But one thing was certain—they were not out here alone.

Xander and Goose were both looking to the east, too,

and Xander was scratching the back of his head. Slocum signaled them both to ease off and hold their fire. If somebody was out there, he wanted to know who they were before he and the Martins started sending a barrage of lead Smollets's way.

He flicked his eyes to the rear to check the horses. Both were waiting exactly where he'd ground-tied them, with Kemo peacefully grazing and Speck looking toward the east, his ears pricked. He knew somebody was coming, too.

The minutes dragged on. Smollets didn't move, not a muscle, and neither did the three men on the ridge. They nervously waited for the shooter to make his appearance. Of course, it might just be somebody out hunting, Slocum thought. There were a few stray miners up this way. But wouldn't they have seen smoke from his fire before now?

Unless he was far from his camp. But why the hell would he need to go far from camp just to hunt? This neck of California was full of game. Many was the time that Slocum had just set up camp in those mountains and waited for the game to wander by.

Which it did—even in the harshest winter—with almost monotonous regularity.

While he was thinking up other reasons to rule out a miner, a mounted rider suddenly appeared on the far eastern ridge, and stopped there. Slocum reached for his collapsible spyglass, which was in his pocket and therefore much easier to get to than the binoculars in his saddlebags. He pulled the spy glass out to its full length and held it to his eye.

"Can't be," he muttered, and then he squinted.

"Can it?" he asked himself, then squinted harder.

Slowly, he began to chuckle. It was. It was old Deputy Grover, or at least it was somebody a lot like him, riding his horse. This was just too much of a coincidence to be one. Prescott must have sent him, and he'd gotten lost going through the mountains. That was a Grover trick, all right.

Slocum shook his head. Grover could get lost crossing the street.

He held his rifle barrel up high and waved it, which caught Grover's attention, but unfortunately Smollets's, too. And Smollets took a shot at Slocum.

He missed, but Slocum felt the quick breeze as Smollets's slug sailed only inches from his hand. He pulled his arm down immediately—just as he heard the shot ring out—then signaled Xander and Goose to hold again.

When he looked back toward the place where Grover had been sitting his horse, he wasn't there anymore.

Damn it anyway! If he'd gone back into those hills to try to come up behind Smollets, or to go back south of Slocum and join them from the rear, he was liable to end up in New York City!

How much longer would this go on? Smollets had sited the man to the east—who was he, anyway?—but he'd disappeared before Smollets had a chance to draw a bead on him. Damn! And now he couldn't decide which way the man had gone. Or if he'd seen him, or Slocum, or the others.

They seemed plain enough to Smollets—on occasion—but perhaps, given the angle . . .

Hell and damnation!

Well, the man was gone now. That was the excuse he'd made for taking that shot at the one he was fairly sure was Slocum. That arm with the rifle had surely gone down in a trice, hadn't it? Perhaps he'd hit him!

That glorious thought was soon erased, however, by reality. Where he'd wanted to hit him was in the head or the chest, and the best he could have done was nip his arm. Blasted horse. Blasted terrain.

He slapped the dead horse again, hoping he'd feel it in the afterlife, if such things applied to horses and beasts. How dare he die right here and now? Why couldn't he have waited until they came to a town?

His figuring put them within fifteen miles of Sacramento. "Couldn't you have waited a little longer?" he spat, and slapped the horse again for good measure.

Suddenly, his shoulder felt like fire and invisible hands shoved him back and off the carcass. It took him about as long to realize he'd been wounded as it took him to hear the shot.

He couldn't say which position the slug had come from. The force of it had knocked him back enough that now he was lying at a different angle than before. But it didn't matter, he told himself as he quickly wrapped his bandana under his armpit and over his shoulder, tying it with fingers and teeth. He wanted to make sure that he lived long enough, at least, to see all of them dead.

Slocum wiped sweat from his forehead and neck, and was as surprised as anyone to hear the bullet sing, and see Smollets thrown back. Smollets was now completely behind the horse, and Slocum could only see his legs.

He glanced toward Goose and Xander, but each signaled that he hadn't done it. He believed them. Therefore, the shot could only have come from—

"Hey there, you old Arkansas razorback!" said a familiar voice.

Slocum flipped over on his back and saw Clint Grover come crawling toward him, rifle in hand. He had the biggest shit-eating grin on his face that Slocum had ever seen there. He grinned right back and said, "Grover! I can't believe they sent you! And that you found us! The U.S. Marshal's Office has come a long way."

Grover crawled up next to him. "Yeah, yeah, rub it in. You're never gonna let me forget how I missed Santa Fe that time, are you?"

Slocum grinned. "Nope."

"So I take it that's Harvey Smollets you got cornered down there?" asked Grover.

"One and the same."

"And that's his dead horse, too, ain't it?"

"Right again."

"You'll be happy to know that's why I clipped him. Know how you can't abide a horse killer, a horse thief, a horse—"

"All right, all right," Slocum said with a crooked grin. "Not gonna let me forget how that son of a bitch we caught in New Mexico had up and swiped my horse, either, are you?"

Grover shook his head. "Not in a million years."

"Comfortin'," said Slocum.

Grover laughed. "So, how you want to do this?"

"You're the law. You tell me."

Grover scratched his chin. "I don't suppose you've tried talkin' him out?"

"Can't see that it'd do any good. He's out for blood. Mine in particular, I guess. He hired a gun to get me—that was back in Lonesome—but I got the drop on him first."

"Smollets or the gun?"

"Now, don't get smart-alecky with me. The gun, of course. Odie Ames."

Grover nodded. "Hope you killed him. We been tryin' to get him for years. Hell, we'd be looking for Smollets for years, too, if you hadn't already practically had him in custody. How's it feel to be doing half the U.S. marshal's work for him?"

Slocum grunted. "I'm underpaid and overworked."

"My feelings exactly. Now, what d'you say we all start shootin' at once and just walk toward him? Don't know how he's feelin', but it'd scare the bejesus outta me!"

Slocum agreed, and they crawled to tell the Martins the plan, such as it was.

"Hell, we could'a did that a long time ago," Goose groused when Slocum told him.

"I know, I know, but he's the law. He says it, we do it,"

Slocum replied. Actually, he figured that one or more of them were going to get shot, but so be it. At least their horses were safe. "On my signal, all right?"

Goose nodded, and Slocum crawled back the way he'd come.

There was movement up on the ridge. Smollets crawled a little forward and up on the horse, his rifle in one hand and his pistol at the ready. At least the slug had hit him in the left shoulder, he thought. At least his gun hand was untouched.

Up high, he watched the hat shift again. Slocum's, he'd bet anything. He took careful aim, held his breath, and fired.

The hat flew skyward, but the top of the head, dark-haired and unbloodied, ducked down and out of sight.

Bloody hell!

13

Damn! Slocum thought as he practically buried himself in the desert floor. He felt his head and sighed with relief. No blood, no wound.

His hat had flown straight up, it seemed, and was resting on a cactus about two steps away. If he'd been standing, that was.

As Grover crawled toward him, he moved down the slope to snag it. It came away stickered with cactus spines, and he swore softly.

"Aw, go ahead," Grover whispered. "Put it on. Maybe it'll stay stuck on this time."

"Real funny," carped Slocum. "You oughta go on the stage."

"And there's one leaving at noon," they said together, then broke out into laughter. The tension's back was broken by it, and they both began to rain bullets down on the man and the dead horse below.

Slocum signaled to the right and Grover signaled to the left, and both Xander and Goose began to fire, too. Slocum and Grover crossed the highest point of the ridge and skit-

tered down it, both firing without cease with their rifles.
Once they'd made it about ten feet down the slope, Xander
and Goose stepped forward, firing like madmen.

The horse's corpse was growing unrecognizable as
Smollets cowered behind it, putting his head against the
girth so he'd have the protection of the saddle as well as
his gelding. He was done for, and he knew it. He'd stopped
firing—or even trying to fire—when the second two men
stepped into sight and down the slope, their guns blazing. It
sounded like there was a whole battalion coming toward
him.

And then it was there. The bullets stopped pounding into
his horse and saddle, pinging off the small rocks and sink-
ing into the sand that surrounded him. He hadn't realized
that he'd closed his eyes, but now he slowly opened them.
And saw boots. Eight dusty boots, worn by four dusty men.
One of which wore a U.S. deputy marshal's badge, and one
of which was Slocum. All four carried rifles, and all four
rifles were barrel-down and aimed at his head.

"Stop your quakin' and stand up, you little shit," said
one of the men he didn't know. He looked like he could be
the father of the young one. At least, both were tall and
redheaded.

Somehow, he made it to his feet. He took a silent inven-
tory as he slowly stood. No other wounds besides his shoulder. This was good. At least, good on the surface. They
could be planning to beat him to death, right here and now.
Or just shoot him.

After all, he'd do it if he were in their place.

Good thing for him that he wasn't.

Smollets stood before them, wounded and cowed. Goose
reached in and grabbed his rifle and handgun while Grover
frisked him for any hidden weapons. He carried none, which
surprised Slocum. He would have thought that a sleazy

little sneak like Smollets would have carried a hideout gun up each sleeve and a dagger in each boot.

At last Xander was dispatched to bring up the horses, which had all but been forgotten in the excitement of the capture. He returned momentarily, leading all five mounts.

Grover saw them coming and said, "I thought two was pushin' the limit, Slocum, but how the hell you ride three'a those things at once is beyond me!"

Xander didn't like his horse being made part of the joke, and quickly said, "Eagle's mine, mister. Only two of them Appys are Slocum's."

His face serious, Grover said, "Pardon my manners, young feller! I can see now that he's too muscled out to belong to Slocum."

Now Xander was really confused. But Slocum came to his rescue. "You callin' my horses skinny, Grover?"

"Sorry, there, buddy," Grover said, trying to hide a smile. "I was just thinkin' out loud that they were a pretty pair. Now, which one is Smollets gonna ride into Sacramento?"

Slocum felt his neck go hot. "Not one'a mine! Let the murderin' horse killer hoof it on his lonesome!"

Grover scratched the back of his neck. "Now, if we do that, I reckon he might just run away."

"You know what I mean," Slocum snapped. "Get moving. Let's cover this horse with brush before we burn him."

Eventually, when the fire was lit and blazing, they all mounted up—a wrist-bound Smollets on Dusty, led on a short rope by Grover, riding Kemo—and moved on north, toward Sacramento.

When they reached Sacramento, Grover checked Smollets in with the local sheriff before he, Slocum, Goose, and Xander all hiked over to the hotel, then the livery, and finally, a restaurant with the imposing name of "Miss Sally Perdue's Grade 'A' Steak House ** Ribs A Specialty."

Goose and Slocum both ordered a thick steak and a rack of ribs, while Xander and Grover held themselves down to one order each—Xander got a steak, while Grover ordered the ribs.

Whoever this Sally Perdue woman was, she sure had a handle on cooking meat, Slocum thought. Her ribs were so tender they were falling off the bone, and her steaks were so tender you could cut them with a fork.

Slocum was about to say something to this effect—the others being so intent on their food that they were incapable of speech—when he thought he heard a familiar voice.

A female familiar voice.

He spun around in his chair and scanned the crowd.

Sitting not three tables away from him was Samantha—Hiram Walker's cook, with whom he'd had a dalliance when they were back in Tucson. Or just outside it, really. For once, he was speechless, and not because his mouth was full of food. He was actually dumbstruck.

As the reality of her presence took hold, he noticed she was seated with another girl, this one younger, who looked a good bit like her. A sister? A cousin? Some kind of relative, he'd bet. But what was she doing here, of all places, so far from home?

Without realizing it, he slowly stood, leaving his table behind and moving toward hers. It seemed he was there in an instant, looking down at her. He could have taken her right there, in front of God and the patrons and everybody.

But instead, he let discretion be the better part of valor. "Sam?" he said softly.

She froze, then turned her face up toward his. An astounded grin suddenly wrapped her beautiful face. "Slocum!" she cried, and leapt to her feet, leapt into his arms. "I missed you so much!" she cried into his shoulder. And when he lifted her chin so that he could look into her eyes, she truly was crying.

"I missed you, too, Sam," he said softly. "But what . . . why are you up here in California?"

"Helping my cousin get her restaurant started. And you?"

He turned her so that she could see his table. "Helpin' Goose and Xander take care of some unfinished business, and helpin' the U.S. Marshal's Office gather up Harvey Smollets."

Sam waved to Goose, who was looking up and elbowing Xander. They both waved back happily, Xander with the most enthusiasm. Grover just kept on eating.

"And this," she said, turning him back toward her table and her dining partner, "is my cousin Sally."

"Pleased," said Slocum, and held out his hand.

"Thank you," she replied, and took it, shaking it enthusiastically. "Sam's been telling me all about you. How you brought back Mr. Walker's stolen cattle, I mean," she said, blushing.

"Would you and your friends care to join us?" Sam asked.

"Why don't we do it the other way round?" Slocum said, and picked up as much of her place setting as he could handle.

She rested her hand on his arm, and he was instantly— and embarrassingly—hard. "It's all right, Slocum," she said, referring to the food. "It's taken care of."

Sally stood, too, and signaled to one of the waiters. He was with them in a flash and she instructed him to move their things. And then, Samantha leading the way (with Slocum close behind), they made their way to Slocum's table, much to the delight of the other men.

It turned out that Sam was staying with Sally, who had a private apartment upstairs. And thankfully, it had two bedrooms.

By the time they finished eating and said good night to the Martins and Grover, Slocum didn't think he could stand it much longer. As it turned out, he didn't have to.

After the lovemaking was over—at roughly two in the morning, since Slocum felt he had to make up for lost time—she nestled under his arm while he toyed with her nipples, and for the first time, they had a chance to talk. She told him that Sheriff Black had been as hopped up as a hornet about the California sheriff's attitude—as well he should have been—but when the U.S. Marshal's Office had said they were sending a man, he had calmed down considerably.

It was then that Hiram had let her take the stage out to California to aid her widowed cousin in getting her steak house up and running, but only if she fixed some meals ahead. She said she'd readied hams and roasts and cakes and pies and everything she could think of that would keep for a few days, and left her brother and his wife in charge of the kitchen.

"Well, I gotta say I can't blame Hiram," Slocum said, smiling. He'd found a place, just to the right of her left nipple, that made her giggle when it was stroked just so. "If you were cookin' for me, I'd never let you outta my sight."

"Oh you wouldn't, would you?" she replied, and punched him playfully in the chest.

"Ouch," he said, laughing.

"So tell me how you caught Smollets. And that other fella you mentioned. Somebody Ames?"

Slocum settled into telling the story, which greatly helped him to get the facts straight in his head. There'd been so much time wasted, he realized. But then, everything happened for a reason, they said. If they hadn't wasted so much time in Lonesome, they wouldn't have gotten Odie Ames, wouldn't have run into ol' Grover this afternoon, nor would they have come across Samantha earlier this evening.

"And that's what happened," he said, finishing the tale. "Then we looked for a good place to eat, and the rest, like they say, is history." He turned toward her slightly, dipped his head, and wrapped his lips around one of her nipples.

"Oh, Slocum, I'm too tired to start again!" she said. "It's almost three in the morning!"

He let go of her nipple and kissed it tenderly. "You're right, baby. We both need some shut-eye, and need it bad." He realized that just recounting the day's adventures had worn him out, and also that he was having a tough time keeping his eyes open.

"That's my boy," Sam whispered, and snuffed out the candle on her side of the bed.

"And that's my gal," Slocum murmured, and reached for his.

They were both asleep within five minutes.

14

When Slocum awoke the next morning, it was in the nicest possible way: Samantha was sucking his cock. By the time he came fully awake, its length and girth had so expanded that she'd given up trying to take him into her mouth, and had begun to lave it with her tongue from base to tip, over and over. He didn't want her to ever stop.

Almost.

He reached down for her and she came kissing her way up his abdomen, his chest, his neck, and finally kissing his lips, long and deep and with great passion. While he returned it hungrily, she slid her legs up to bracket his rib cage, her knees even with his nipples and her wet, hot, opening positioned just at the eager tip of his rock-hard member.

"Sam . . ." Slocum moaned, feeling, for once, as if he'd been entirely taken over in the best possible way. "Sam . . ."

She responded by backing her hips up, then down, until she'd completely enveloped him in her moist warmth, and she sighed at the same time he did.

And then, she slowly began to move upon him, propping her torso on her hands so that he could play with her breasts when she wasn't dipping her face down to kiss him. She chose her own meter, danced to her own internal music.

For Slocum it was a revelation, being so passive, letting her run the show, but she was doing it so perfectly that he had no quibbles whatsoever. He simply went along, taking his cues from her.

And then she sat up straight, constantly riding him so that he could see himself sliding in and out of her, glistening with her moisture. He imagined steam coming from their juncture, she was moving so feverishly, and then he couldn't think at all. He put a hand on each of her thighs as if he were hanging on for dear life. And he came, as explosively as he ever remembered, bucking up into her uncontrollably and with some sort of sound, primal and almost unidentifiable as coming from his mouth.

She came at the same time, and he saw that her head was thrown back, all the cords in her neck standing out and her mouth opening in a silent scream.

Moments later, she collapsed, panting, onto his chest, head against his shoulder, as if she had no more energy for kisses or even speech.

He understood completely. Still embedded deep within her and feeling her internal contractions rhythmically massage him, he simply wrapped her in his arms and held her while he buried his face in the fragrance of her soft and abundant sable curls.

Smollets did not wake to circumstances nearly so pleasant as Slocum. At least he was in a cell by himself, but that was the only thing good he could think of about it. The walls were brick and he had no window. The cell door was not bars, but solid wood, with a slot only wide and tall enough for the guard to shove a meal tray through, and at eye level, an iron-barred opening only slightly larger than a man's face.

He was screwed, and he knew it. He'd never escape

from this place. His only hope was to somehow slip free of the deputy marshal on the way back to Arizona. The question was . . . how?

It was this problem that he was examining when the guard brought his breakfast. Bread and beans. How thrilling.

He got down as much of it as he could, figuring he'd need the energy later, then pushed his tin plate aside and went back to plotting and planning.

Goose was excited to be so near to his home, and Xander shared his enthusiasm—there were three half sisters he had yet to meet, plus a stepmother! He only hoped they would accept him as he planned on accepting them—with open arms. He was full of questions, with which he peppered Goose from the moment they woke that morning.

Goose was a little surprised by the interrogation, to be frank. He just figured he'd take the boy home, they'd accept him, and that would be that. But it seemed like the kid wanted to make it as complicated as possible.

Was there an extra stall for Eagle? Was the house close to town? Would he have a room of his own? Did Goose have a dog? On and on.

Goose finally decided the best course was to wire his wife, Mariska, that he was in Sacramento, and that he was bringing home Xander. It took him a while to figure out how to explain Xander in ten words or less, but then he remembered the extra cash Slocum had handed them back in Arizona, and realized he could afford to send a more lengthy explanation.

He was still unsure of the wording when he gave up and sent it off, but he'd been working on it an hour and he hadn't had any breakfast yet. His stomach won out.

He didn't recall until later on in the morning that he hadn't mentioned Slocum coming along, and had to send another wire—this one, much shorter.

In between visits to the telegrapher's office, they hiked back over to Sally's, hoping that she'd be open for breakfast, too. On the way, they ran across Grover, who had the same quest on his mind.

The three of them found Sally's not only open, but doing a booming business.

They were waiting to be seated when Xander spotted Slocum, sitting with Sam and her cousin Sally across the room. Xander waved and hollered, catching Slocum's attention, and Slocum waved them over.

Goose thought Slocum looked awfully cozy with the gal from Arizona—Hiram Walker's cook—but said nothing. The three of them—Goose, Xander, and Grover—all found chairs and pulled them up hungrily.

"What do you recommend, Miss Sally?" Grover asked shyly.

Great, Goose thought. Seemed like those gals were real magnets for men. Anyway, men he was riding with.

Sally called over a waiter and ordered for all three of them. As it turned out, she must have ordered the same for Slocum, her cousin Sam, and herself, too. They all feasted on fried ham and applesauce, fried potatoes and bacon, thick Texas toast with cactus jelly and fresh butter, scrambled eggs with jalapeno peppers, real homemade Danish pastries, and what seemed like gallons of hot coffee.

And when they were at last finished, it was all Goose could do to walk to the door. He slumped down on a bench at one side of the front door and said, "Xander, it's gonna take me a few minutes to get myself up and runnin' again."

He pulled a scrap of paper and a pencil from his pocket and scribbled something on it, then handed it over. "Take this to the telegraph office and send it to the same address where I sent the first one. All right?"

"Sure!" said Xander, and scurried off, up the street.

Slocum looked at Goose and cocked a brow.

"Aw, hell," Goose said. "I already wired Mariska about

Xander and everythin', but I forgot to tell her you was comin', too."

Slocum laughed. "I'm not most people's favorite surprise."

Samantha bumped him softly with her hip and said, "You're mine, Slocum."

Grover had decided to put off his return to Arizona long enough to see the Pacific Ocean, and had wired his intentions to Prescott. Marshal Egan himself had wired back, telling him to have a good time. Well, he guessed you couldn't get a bigger go-ahead than that! After breakfast, he made his way to the local jail and told the marshal there of his intentions. He got their permission, too.

Life would be a lot easier, he told himself, if he were more like Slocum, going wherever the wind blew. But then he remembered that Slocum didn't have a savings account or a pension, and thought of it no more.

He picked up Sally—whom he'd parked on an office bench while he saw the marshal—and the two of them set off, arm in arm, to see the city.

Once Goose recovered from breakfast, he was all for leaving town right away. Two things stopped him, though. For one, Xander was missing. And for two, so was Slocum. They'd just vanished into thin air. Even when he went back to the hotel, they were nowhere to be found.

Puzzled, Goose lay down to think about it—and didn't wake up until mid-afternoon.

Xander, after a lengthy trip to the penny candy aisle of the closest general store, had journeyed over to Table's Livery, where he'd seen an advertisement for a small rodeo. He bought a ticket and went inside, figuring to find a corral and a bull or two, and maybe a couple of bucking horses. But he found an enormous arena, backed with paddock after paddock of livestock.

Thrilled, he found a seat in the bleachers and spent the afternoon nibbling his candy and cheering the bull and bucking horse riders, the barrel racers and the bulldoggers and the ropers, and all the others.

By six o'clock, he was exhausted. And, he also realized, starving. As the light started to die and the rodeo commenced its closing ceremonies, Xander began the long walk back to Sally's café. Those ribs—and their barbeque sauce—were calling to him!

At about the same time Xander was heading back to the café, Slocum and Samantha were just waking from a postcoital doze. This had to be one of the best afternoons Slocum had spent in quite some time. And it became even better when, as they were dressing for dinner, Samantha suddenly and tearfully announced that tomorrow she was leaving for San Francisco.

"I have to go," she sobbed. "Mr. Walker expects, he expects . . ." She collapsed into tears.

Slocum was already at her side. "Don't cry, baby," he said soothingly. "We're heading out, too."

She sniffed and raised her head. "And stopping in San Francisco?"

He grinned, nodding.

"Oh, Slocum! You're a miracle!" She threw her arms around him and hugged him as tightly as she could.

He just smiled dumbly.

Smollets was, at about that time, receiving his dinner tray. Up went the slot door, in came a tray, and that was it. No "Good evening" or even "How ya doin'?" *Personable rapscallions, these Sacramento jailers, blast them to perdition!*

Tonight's menu was bread, beans, a thin slice of ham, and coffee, reasonably hot. None of which struck a note with him—except for the coffee cup.

He measured the width of his hand alongside the mug.

His hand was somewhat smaller than the cup was tall, and he smiled.

With greatly heightened spirits, he ate his dinner, drank his coffee, put the tray back on the little ledge next to the slot, and waited.

His expression was self-satisfied.

When the jailer finally came to retrieve the tray, Smollets was quick. The second the door slid up, his left hand was through the opening, punching the guard in the gut as hard as he could. He automatically reached for the man's belt as he doubled over and just managed to catch it as he pushed his right hand through, too, to help.

In this clumsy fashion, he went through the man's pockets as well as he could, and finally found a ring of keys attached to the back of his belt. Getting it free was one problem, but finding the keyhole was another. The locking mechanism seemed to be a one-sided affair, and after he let the guard's body tumble to the floor outside, it took him as much time to find the keyhole and latch as it did to find the right key.

But he did, finally, and dragged the still-unconscious guard inside the cell, taking care not to let the door swing closed.

And then there was getting out to reckon with. He remembered the way they had brought him in, so he reversed the procedure in his mind and crept along the corridors, unseen and unheard by guard or prisoner. They must have had a very low escape rate here to be so confident—no guards were posted.

At long last he came to a door leading outside. Again, not a guard in sight. He tried opening it.

The door was locked. Immediately, an alarm bell started to clang.

Drat!

15

But the clatter of footsteps he was expecting did not come. Frantically, he searched through the ring of keys he'd taken from the guard, looking for something different, something brass. The lock appeared to be made of it and so should the key, he reckoned.

Quickly, he flipped through the keys until he found what he was looking for. This had better be it, he thought, for the sound of approaching footsteps was growing near.

He jammed the key in the lock, closed his eyes, and turned it.

It worked!

He slipped out the door and pulled it closed behind him, then quickly raced up the alley he'd emerged upon. The street was full of traffic, and he slowed his pace to blend in as he moved away from the building, adjusting his clothes as he went. He threw off his jacket, pushed up his shirt-sleeves, and purposely mussed his hair. To appear to be a working man, going home at the close of day—that was his goal.

By the time he'd walked to the next corner, he imagined

that even his own mother wouldn't recognize him. And he was right. The man who had gone into jail dressed as a dandy was now scruffy and unshaved, with ripped clothing.

He smelled faintly of urine, too.

He kept on walking until he found himself next to a small livery, closed for the evening. It was no problem to walk around to the back, slip in a stall window, pick out and saddle a horse, then ride him out the back door.

He didn't move out at a canter until he'd reached the edge of the city. He was going south, to San Francisco. Even if Slocum could follow him there, he'd never find him. San Francisco was too big, too busy. A place where a man could get himself lost, if he wanted.

And he wanted it.

He also wanted—no, needed—some cash. They'd stripped him of all his worldly goods at the jail, blast them. They'd reduced him to common street crime, just to survive!

While he considered his possibilities—or lack thereof—he galloped off.

"So, you takin' the stage or you gonna ride?" Grover asked Samantha around a mouthful of ribs.

"Since I don't have a horse, I think the stage would be more appropriate," Sam replied with a smile. Beneath the table, her hand was on Slocum's thigh.

Slocum sat up. "Hell, Sam, I got two horses. 'Less Grover needs one to carry his prisoner, that is . . ."

"Nope!" said Grover, chewing. "Told 'em when I took Smollets in that I was bound to see the Pacific Ocean, and I didn't much feel like havin' him tag along. They're takin' him. Two marshals. On the train." He paused to swallow. "Day after tomorrow," he finished.

"Well, hot damn!" Slocum cheered. "Sam, you're comin' with us!"

Her face lit up. "I'd love to, Slocum!" She paused. "That

is, if you don't feel that a woman would get in your way . . ."

"Get in the way?" he asked. "Why, if you'll just cook the suppers along the trail, you can get in the way all you want!"

Everybody at the table laughed. That was, until a tall, blond beanstalk of a deputy marshal, bedraggled and recognizable only by his badge, came in the front door and made his way to their table. Panting, he said, "Marshal Grover?"

"That's the name, Marshal . . .?"

"Kellaway," the man said, still out of breath.

The table behind them had just cleared, and Xander grabbed an empty chair and spun it around for the marshal.

"Thanks, kid," the man said, then slouched down into it. He turned his attention back to Grover. "I'm bringin' you bad news, I'm afraid."

Grover's brow furrowed. "Go on."

"That prisoner you brought in yesterday? Harvey Smollets . . ." Kellaway put a hand to his face, then dragged his fingers down one stubbly cheek. "He's escaped."

"Son of a bitch!" snorted Slocum. "Didn't you warn them about him, Grover?!"

"Apparently they didn't listen," said Grover, still looking at Kellaway.

"But we did!" Kellaway argued. "We put him in a cell with no window, either to the outside or the hall. And no key locks on the inside. He got his meals through a slot in the door, and nobody was to talk to him, no matter what."

Slocum shook his head. "Didn't work, did it?"

Kellaway shook his head sadly, and with no small degree of embarrassment. "We still don't know what happened. The guard went to retrieve the dinner trays and woke up locked in Smollets's cell. That's all he can remember."

"He's lucky he can remember anything," Slocum muttered. "Lucky to be breathin'. Man already killed an old woman."

Grover asked, "Any idea which way he went? Or how the hell he's gettin' there?"

"Not on any'a your horses," Kellaway said quickly. "We already posted guards."

"Good," said Slocum. The last thing he wanted was to think about slimy Harvey Smollets riding one of his good horses to death. "And you've come to tell us this . . . why?"

"Well, I figured you havin' brought him in and all, you'd want to join in the hunt for him!" Kellaway said, a little shocked.

Slocum didn't waste any time. He said, "There you'd be wrong, Marshal," and shoved a bite of ribs in his mouth.

Kellaway looked perplexed. Goose turned away from him, and Xander, too. Grover had the grace to at least shrug his shoulders before he turned back to his supper.

Slowly, Kellaway stood up. "Sorry to bother you folks durin' your supper," he said, and started to make his way out.

But just before he reached the door, Grover shouted at him. "Kellaway!" He turned round to face the table, a glimmer of hope in his eyes.

Grover said, "We're headed out, down San Francisco way. We'll keep our eyes open, all right?"

Kellaway's face fell, but he accepted the offer, saying, "Thanks, Marshal Grover," and tipping his hat as he left the restaurant.

"Well, shit," grumbled Goose, which just about covered the conversation for everybody at the table.

Slocum muttered, "Amen to that!" and dug back into his supper.

The next morning, Slocum kissed Samantha good-bye—temporarily—then set out to meet the three other men at the livery. They were already there when he arrived, getting their horses ready.

He was pleased to see that they were all present and accounted for—the men and the horses, both. Goose, picking out Kip's rear hind hoof, told Slocum that the deputies had just left. This made him happy, too. There were very few members of the marshal's office that he could stand, let alone that he'd ride with. Grover, currently wiping down his horse's face, was one exception.

When they had all mounted up, they rode back to Sally's restaurant to pick up Sam. Sally wasn't coming, much to Grover's disappointment. But he'd promised to ride back her way once he'd seen the ocean, and she'd promised to be there. Slocum could see a romance in Grover's future. And her cooking would put some meat on his bones, too.

Samantha was ready and waiting out front with one small bag and one medium: the most Slocum had said she could take along. While he was loading her horse and shortening the stirrups, a familiar face appeared in the crowd—Deputy Kellaway.

"Mornin', folks!" he said, touching the brim of his hat. "Ladies." He looked up at Samantha, then Sally, who was back beside the building, saying good-bye to Grover.

Sam smiled at him. "Good morning, Deputy. What can we do for you?"

"Just glad to see you folks've still got your horses, miss," he replied. "Came to tell you that we found out what we think he rode out on."

That got Slocum's full attention. He turned around. "What?"

"Bay gelding, about fifteen hands, no white," Kellaway said. "Horse was stole from another livery last evening. We know, 'cause they was closed from five-thirty to seven-thirty with no guard on duty. Horse was there when he locked up, and gone when he got back. Thief crawled through a window and left by the back door. Didn't take nothin' but the horse and gear, and headed out goin' south. Didn't even steal grain."

"Figures," muttered Slocum. He felt sorry for the horse, even if he'd never laid an eye on him.

He caught Goose staring at him from the corner of his eye and, reading the unspoken question there, said, "No."

Goose shrugged and dropped his eyes.

Good thing Goose didn't press him, because Slocum was half-tempted to take out after the murdering, horse-thieving bastard.

Instead, though, he made sure Samantha was set and ready on Kemo, then mounted Speck. The horses were ready to go, and Speck snorted in anticipation.

The others were ready. Slocum nodded what he hoped would be a final good-bye to Kellaway, said, "We'll keep our eyes peeled, Marshal," and then turned to the bulk of his own traveling companions. "Let's move out." He figured that if they kept up a reasonable pace, they might make San Francisco by midday, the following day.

Smollets was already halfway there. He had learned something from the previous horse, at least. He had stopped three times, so far, to let the gelding graze and drink. This was his fourth stop.

He had come to a treeless place filled with rolling hills, most of which were covered in grass and clover, and found a small stream trickling between a few of them. He'd watered the horse, then changed its bridle for a halter attached to a long rope. He plunked himself down on a boulder and let the horse go to work mowing the grass.

He figured it was in his best interest to keep the horse fit, not only in the interest of continued transport, but because he figured to be able to sell it once he got to San Francisco. That would give him a little "running money," anyway.

Also, he had an account at a bank in San Francisco.

There wasn't much cash in it—just two hundred dollars—and he'd opened the account under an assumed name, but it was a tad more with which to start anew. Actually, he'd forgotten about the account until last night, when he was fleeing the local constabulary in Sacramento.

It was difficult to remember all the details when your life was suddenly turned upside down by circumstances beyond your control.

Like that idiot, Slocum.

He ground his teeth, then made himself stop. He'd grind them down to nubs if he let himself.

He checked his pocket watch—or rather, the pocket watch he'd found in the horse's saddlebags. It was old, made of nickel plate over some base metal, not gold, and for all he knew, lost fifteen minutes every hour of the day. But it was all he had.

It read eight-forty-five. He decided to give the horse another fifteen minutes to graze.

16

Smollets wasn't exactly rolling in money, but he felt better. For the time being. Upon entering town, he had suddenly realized that he not only had little money, he had none. And he asked directions to the nearest horse trader.

He sold the horse for fifty-five dollars (although he thought he'd been taken), claiming the reason he had no sales receipt was that he'd had the horse since it was foaled. But he got twenty-five dollars for the tack, which helped him feel better.

He inquired about the nearest clean hotel, and received directions to go back down the street and turn left. He found the hotel immediately, took a room—signing the register Ambrose Wellington—and then sat down at his room's little desk and began to forge himself identification documents. It was an old game of his, and he finished with papers that not only looked official, but appeared suitably aged.

After grabbing a sandwich at the downstairs café, he

went to bed, satisfied that come morning, he'd have no trouble at the bank.

Slocum woke next to Samantha, and it took him a second to remember where he was: in San Francisco, in a hotel, after arriving earlier this morning. Samantha made a sleep sound deep in her throat beside him, and cuddled closer. He put his arm around her.

Let her sleep as long as she wants, he thought, brushing a stray lock of hair out of her face. *She's been a trouper.*

She had, too, and last night she had cooked them probably the best trailside dinner in the history of the universe: chicken and noodles and carrots and potatoes and apple streusel and butter she'd brought along, plus wild onions, chokecherries, roasted pine nuts, and a couple of rabbits that they'd shot along the trail. He was still full. Well, not really. He could use some lunch. And he started thinking about where they'd passed cafés and restaurants on their way into town.

Grover had reminded them that San Francisco had gun laws—nothing beyond the city limits—so Slocum had taken off his Colt sidearm and was planning to wear only his cross-draw rig. It could easily be hidden by a coat or jacket. In this case, it'd have to be his old duster. It was all he had with him, but it'd so the trick. Besides, San Francisco was some chillier than Southern California or Arizona had been. He wouldn't look out of place. He hoped that Goose had a backup plan, too. He knew that Grover would have one. Xander? Well, that was a wild card.

He hadn't forgotten about Smollets, either. When they went to the livery yesterday, he'd checked all the boarders out. Nothing plain bay was in the place. Well, so much for one out of . . . How many liveries were there in San Francisco, anyhow?

Probably hundreds.

He scowled, then suddenly felt Sam's fingers on his lips. He kissed them. "Awake?"

"Enough to see you making that grumbly face," she whispered. "Why so glum?"

"It's nothing," he said, glossing over his thoughts. It didn't concern her, anyway. "Feel like some lunch?"

In reply, her stomach growled, and she laughed. "I guess that answers your question, Slocum."

He guessed it did, too. He stood up, then offered her his hand. "Let's get duded up, then," he said, smiling. "We're in the Big City now!"

Grover woke before Goose and Xander, and was dressed by the time that Xander cracked an eyelid.

"Why're you up so early?" the kid asked, his voice full with the grogginess of sleep. "What time is it, anyway?"

The curtains were drawn, and the room was deep in shadow.

"It's about one in the afternoon," Grover whispered, tipping his head toward Goose, who was still sleeping soundly. And thankfully, not snoring.

Xander pulled himself up to a sitting position. "You thinkin' 'bout havin' some lunch?"

Grover grinned. Leave it to the kid. "Yeah," he said, "I am."

"Wait for me!" Xander said loudly, waking Goose, who sat up straight.

"What?" he said. "What's goin' on?"

Xander, reaching for his gun, said, "Breakfast, if you hurry up!"

Grover held up his hand. "What'd I tell you yesterday about firearms?"

"Oh, yeah . . ." Xander hung his gunbelt on the bed's footboard. "Jeez, Louise!"

"I know, I know," said Grover. "It's a pain in the ass."

Xander scowled. Then, noticing something, he said accusingly, "How come you're wearin' one?"

Grover flipped back the lapel of his jacket. "I'm official. You're not."

Groggily, Goose said, "He's right, son. Now, me? I got a hideout gun."

"Well, get it hid out and let's go eat," Grover said with a laugh.

Just then, there was a rap on the door. Grover, being the closest, opened it. It was Slocum and Samantha, all dressed up—relatively speaking—and ready to go.

"Lunch, anybody?" Slocum asked.

"Give us 'bout ten minutes, Slocum," said Goose.

Slocum nodded. "Meet you downstairs in the lobby, fellas."

"Later, gentlemen," said Samantha, peeking from under Slocum's arm, and giving a warm little wave.

Harvey Smollets was awake and two hundred dollars richer.

The clerk at the bank hadn't questioned the identification he'd offered, and he was happy to give the name of his hotel as his temporary residence. After all, they only knew him by the name he'd given, which was the same name he'd put on the horse's bill of sale, identical to the one under which he had the account: Ambrose Wellington.

He'd stopped by a tailor's and found a suit—a perfect fit right off the rack, and he got a deal on it, to boot—which he bought along with a couple of extra shirts, some undergarments, and a few nice, linen handkerchiefs, which he would pick up tomorrow. They were being monogrammed with his new initials.

He was feeling very full of himself at the moment, and trying to decide what line to go into. Banking was a possibility, but an outside contender. In order to be in line to run one, you had to be the boss's son. Or son-in-law. And he really didn't want to get married to secure his position. Although he didn't completely rule out the possibility. After all, he'd gotten married years ago in New York City—what was her name? Shirley?—to secure a good position in a brokerage firm, and more recently in Chicago—Irene that time, he was fairly certain—to get into the meat packing business.

Neither the jobs nor the women had suited him, and he absented himself within a year in both cases.

As the saying went, third time was the charm—but he put no faith in those old saws. He'd not put his future in the hands of some woman again. No matter how ugly and desperate she was, he thought, thinking briefly of Irene.

He shuddered, and moved on.

He had walked another block when he saw something ahead of him that made him duck into the first alley he found. Slocum and his merry little band were coming down the walk toward him, and he secreted himself behind a stack of packing crates until they passed him, and for some time thereafter.

Couldn't he catch a break? That rotten philistine Slocum was like a bloodhound: always on his trail, always on the scent, always showing up at the worst possible moment!

His good mood ruined, Smollets hiked up the street, went to his hotel room, and locked himself inside to pout.

The group repaired to a decent enough restaurant, where they were served a so-so meal. It was disappointing, but Slocum figured anything would have been a letdown when it was compared to Sam's cooking.

Afterward, over coffee, he asked what the others had planned for the rest of the afternoon. Samantha had errands to run, but waved off Slocum's offer to accompany her. "I know exactly where I'm going and what I need, and I can have the parcels sent to the hotel. What are you boys gonna do? As if I didn't know . . ."

Grover's face bloomed into a grin. "I don't know about

the rest of you fellers, but I'm gonna see me the Pacific Ocean!"

Slocum asked, "Docks or beach?"

"Huh?"

"You wanna go down to the beach or over to the docks?"

"Which is better?"

"Both about the same, if you ask me," Goose offered.

"Unless you wanna go wadin' or swimmin'," said Xander.

"Swimmin'?" asked Goose, brows raised. "Are you crazy, boy?"

Xander furrowed his brow. "Huh?"

"I can see you ain't been around the ocean either, boy," Goose said. "There's things in there that ain't in rivers or lakes. Monsters. Critters that can and will eat you or kill you or both."

Grover sat forward. "You're joshin' us, Goose. Ain't you?"

"'Fraid not. There's things you can't imagine, even after you've seen 'em for yourself. There's whales bigger than a freight car, giant kraken that rise from the deep to snare unwary sailors, monstrous eels, sharks with razors for teeth and a hunger for men—"

Slocum held up his hand. "Goose. You're scarin' the women and children."

He was right. Xander's eyes were bugging out of his head, and Samantha was looking paler and paler. Xander was clear at the other end of the table and beyond his reach, but Slocum put his arm about Sam's shoulders and gave her a comforting little hug.

"W-what's a kraken?" Xander asked.

"Somethin' you don't ever want to meet up with, son," Goose said. He looked like he enjoyed a little too much tossing a scare into the table-side group.

Slocum said, "Goose, I never asked you. You make your living from the sea?"

Goose nodded. "Got a fishing boat," he said proudly. "Crew of seven."

"They out now?"

"Nope, not in summer. Fish go bad real quick, Slocum. Winter's best for shippin' 'em. We get ice from up in the mountains," he added, as if it were an afterthought.

Slocum was a little surprised that Goose hadn't spent his whole life in the saddle, and said so.

"Oh, you're part right, there, Slocum," he said. "My daddy was a cowpuncher all his life, so I was born to it, you might say. But then I met Mariska and her pa, and they kinda got me lookin' at things a little different. So now I'm an independent fisherman with contracts to fill. Kinda boggles the brain, don't it?"

Slocum nodded slowly. Boggle? Indeed, it did.

17

After Slocum got Samantha set off on her errands, he and Goose led the others west, toward the beach, to a place Goose knew where they would actually find the beach, and not dead-end on a rocky cliff overlooking it.

Finally, they came to a place where there *was* a rocky cliff, and Slocum was about to cuss out Goose, when he pointed to the beginnings of a wooden staircase. They made their way down the structure—Slocum had Goose go first, figuring that if it'd hold him, it'd hold anything—and the first thing that overcame Grover was how much sand there was.

"How many wagonloads did they need to bring it all down?" he asked, incredulously, and was dumbfounded when Goose told him that nobody brought it, it just came that way.

But next, they got him to look up at the water. He nearly fell down, amazed at the vastness of it. "You can't see the other side!" Grover breathed. "It just goes on . . . forever!"

"Yeah, yeah," muttered Slocum. And he lifted Grover, who had sunk down to his knees, back on his feet. "Let's go down to the water."

They walked down through the sand. Since it was chilly out, they were the only ones on the beach, except for a picnicking couple about a hundred feet to the south. They, at least, had had the sense to build a bonfire, Slocum noted.

When they reached the water's edge, Grover just started to plow in, until Slocum grabbed his arm and pulled him back. "Take off your boots. And socks, if you've got 'em," he said.

"Oh," said Grover, too excited to really listen. But he walked back a few feet, sat down, and tugged off his boots and socks.

The smell was such that the rest of them moved upwind a few feet.

"I can't believe it!" Grover kept repeating. "I just can't believe it! The real, honest-to-God Pacific Ocean!"

Goose, feeling a little more kindly than the others, just laughed. "Go on, Grover," he said with a chuckle. "Go get them toes wet. Just don't go out too far."

Grover needed no further urging. He walked down to the water, noting his own footprints in the sand, then into it, immediately gripping his shoulders from the temperature. It was cool out, and Slocum figured the water had to be about twenty degrees colder than the air.

But Grover didn't seem to mind much. At one point, he bent and cupped a hand, dipping it into the water and bringing a palmful to his lips. Before Slocum or Goose could shout, "No!" he had taken a mouthful—and rapidly spat it out.

"By God, they were right. It is salty!"

"Damn fool," Goose muttered beneath his breath.

Slocum breathed, "Idiot, more like."

Xander, sitting cross-legged in the sand behind them, said nothing. Well, nothing that either of them heard, anyway.

And that, aside from a close call with a drifting jellyfish, was the sum and total of Grover's experience with the sea.

It seemed to be fine with him, though. All the way back

to the hotel, he went on and on about it, how the sand had felt between his toes, and how the waves were so big, the horizon so vast, and the sea went on and on and on forever . . . Slocum, who'd been tired of this before it got started, bit his tongue and tried not to listen.

But Goose was getting a big kick out of it. Of course, he would, being a "man of the sea" and all . . .

Slocum snorted and shook his head. And just kept on walking.

By the time they got back to the hotel, people were already delivering packages from Sam's little shopping spree. Most, Slocum noted, were from mercantiles—probably food and spices that she couldn't find in Tucson—and some were from Chinatown. Sam was going to cook Chinese food for Hiram? Now, that was a new twist.

He left the packages downstairs where he found them, tipping the attendant an extra two bucks to keep an eye on them, and they all went upstairs to Goose's room.

It was four-thirty in the afternoon. He figured that Sam ought to be showing up pretty soon, to go to dinner, so he had a smoke with Goose, then headed up the hall to check to see if she had returned.

She hadn't.

He sat down in the armchair, stretched out his legs, and rolled himself another quirlie. By the time he was finished, it was nearly five, and he was getting concerned about Sam. He shouldn't have let her go out gallivanting without protection. Meaning him.

He stood up and started pacing, without realizing he was doing it. He only knew he was up and walking when he heard a key in the door.

"Sam!" he said happily, and scooped her up in his arms.

She laughed. "My goodness! If that's the kind of welcome you give when a girl's been shopping, I'll have to remember to do it more often!"

"When she's late for dinner, more like," he said. Then, "Ready?" He offered his arm.

"Ready." She took it, and they went down the hall to collect Goose, Xander, and Grover.

Slocum let Sam pick the restaurant, and was glad that he did. She chose a little Italian place, Antonio's, a few blocks north of the hotel. Slocum was leery at first, and Goose had a hard time making himself walk through the front door, but what they found inside was tremendous.

Veal parmesan, spaghetti with meatballs, lasagne, ravioli, spaghetti with clam sauce, scampi, and on and on: they had it all, and then some. Slocum found himself totally enchanted with pasta. He'd had noodles before, naturally, but this Italian kind was out of this world!

Nobody had to wonder what Xander thought, since he went through three entrees in no time flat, and then ordered an Italian ice for dessert. Goose and Grover plowed in enthusiastically, too. Goose favored the veal, Grover favored the spaghetti with clam sauce. But that didn't stop either of them from ordering a second entree.

Samantha had only the lasagne, but seemed to be getting a kick out of her "Italian cowboy" escorts.

Everybody was so busy eating and laughing and having a good time, that not one of them noticed a slicked-up Harvey Smollets as he passed the window. He didn't notice them, either.

Had he done so, he might have broken into a dead run.

Smollets had decided that San Francisco held nothing for him. This, after mulling it over for an entire afternoon. He decided that he needed some place new, some place booming, some place where he could wheedle his way into a new enterprise, then make it soar for him. Or at least, make it take on the appearance of soaring long enough for someone to buy him out.

He had decided on Seattle. It was fairly new, and nobody from Arizona would ever think to look for him up there, he reasoned. No mining, no livestock, but he thought he could make something work by brokering fish and seafood. After all, he was British. Weren't they all born knowing seafood?

"Certainly!" he exclaimed as he opened the door to the stage depot and approached the counter.

"I want the first thing you have going north," he said. "To Seattle."

The bored clerk said, as if by rote, "You realize you gotta go all the way around the Bay, right?" He pointed to a map on the wall to make his point. "It'll add a couple extra days to the trip."

Smollets let out an impatient sigh. "Isn't there a ferry or something?"

"Or something. Joe Riggs runs his boat this late, but you ain't gonna find nothing else till morning."

"All right, I'll take Mr. Riggs's conveyance. Is there another stage depot on the other side?"

"Yeah, but not much'a one," said the clerk, yawning. "You gotta buy your ticket here."

Scowling, Smollets dug into his pocket. "How much?" he asked, locating his wallet.

The clerk told him and he paid, only to find out that the depot offered rides to the docks—at a price.

"Fine!" Smollets shouted, shelling out more coins. "Just fine. A pack of robbers, that's what you are!"

"No, sir, I believe you're thinkin' of the Butterfield. We here at Wells Fargo are on the up-and-up."

Smollets spat, "Bah!" before he hauled himself outside and found the coach waiting to take passengers to the docks.

He climbed aboard and, after waiting for fifteen minutes (and another passenger), was taken to the docks. Wells Fargo had a covered bench there, out of the wind, where they were asked to sit and wait. Joe Riggs, they were told, would come for them when he arrived.

And that was how Smollets spent his evening—on a cold bench with a stranger, waiting for a boat.

Back at the hotel, Slocum opened the room's door for Samantha, and let her precede him through the opening.

"How gallant!" she said with a smile, and then sat down on the edge of the bed. "Sit down for a second, Slocum."

He started to join her on the bed, but she pointed at the chair. "There, please?"

His brow furrowing, Slocum took the chair, then leaned forward, his elbows on his knees. "What is it, Sam?"

She took a deep breath, then said, "I have to go back home. Tomorrow, Slocum."

For a moment, he just sat there, in a state of shock. He'd been so happy to have her there that he hadn't even considered the possibility of her leaving. Ever!

Finally, he said, "Tomorrow, Sam?"

"In the morning, if possible." She looked at her lap. "I'm so sorry. I tried to tell you earlier, but I just . . ."

He said, "It's all right, Sam. I understand. You've got a job to get back to. Poor ol' Hiram is probably goin' crazy without you around to run his servants and his kitchen."

"Now, Slocum . . ."

He shot to his feet. "Don't 'Now, Slocum' me! How long have you known?"

"Always. I always knew who I worked for. So did you."

Slocum opened his mouth, but nothing came out. Finally, saying, "I'll be back," he left, slamming the door behind him.

Downstairs, outside, he paced the sidewalk. What was wrong with her? No, what the hell was wrong with him?! She was right, and he knew it. How long had he been planning to say the same thing to her? And how many other women had he said it to before?

He sat down on a bench with a thump and stuck his legs out onto the walk.

But he'd never felt this way.

Yes, he had. Twice before. He'd nearly fallen, nearly proposed, and what happened when he came to the next town? He found himself a pretty young thing and forgot about the girl he'd loved.

He told himself that he was lousy husband material, and that was most certainly the truth. He told himself that he'd survived these many years without a ball and chain. He told himself that he could forget her, just like the two before her.

And he told himself that he'd better get his butt upstairs and apologize pretty damned fast, if he expected to have himself a decent night.

He did.

18

The next morning found Smollets well on his way to Seattle, and Slocum and company helping to load Samantha's purchases on the stage. There were quite a few.

"If you don't mind me askin'," Goose ventured as he labored with a heavy crate, "just what you got in here, Samantha?"

"Of course I don't, Goose," she replied. "Pots and pans we needed, spices they don't carry in Tucson, canned foods. Things like that."

Slocum was still sorry to see her go, but also still puzzled by the Chinese box. "You gonna start cookin' Chinese for Hiram?"

She laughed. "I doubt he'd stand for it. But his wife likes special teas, and the occasional fortune cookie, or dinner made in a wok."

"What's a 'wok'?" asked Xander.

"It's a special kind of pot that only the Chinese use," Sam replied. She joined her arms in a circle and said, "About this big around and without a flat bottom, like regular pans. You use it for frying or steaming."

Xander still didn't seem to get it, but Sam turned her attention back to the loading. Slocum had just got the last box situated, and Goose was up top, tying everything down.

He said, "That oughta do it, ma'am," tying off the last knot. He climbed down to join them.

The driver motioned to her to get in. She put her foot on the step, then turned toward Slocum. "Come to Tucson again, Slocum. Soon, all right?"

He smiled and took her in his arms. "It's a deal, Sam," he whispered before he kissed her, a kiss long enough to last.

When they were finished, she hopped into the stage, Slocum closed the door behind her, and the driver cracked his whip.

Slocum stood there quite a while, watching the stage disappear into the distance.

"Slocum? Hey, Slocum!" said a voice at his elbow. Grover. He was looking a tad befuddled.

Slocum looked around. The same look of bewilderment was on the faces of all his comrades. He'd best pull himself together, he thought. Wouldn't do to get all emotional in front of the men. Course, he thought Goose might understand, but Goose was only one out of three.

Slocum said, "Well, let's get on over to the livery stable, boys." He stepped out, full of purpose.

One thing that Slocum still hadn't figured out was what to do with Kemo. Sure, he could sell him to a horse trader, but what future would the gelding have then? Being ridden into the ground by some idiot like Smollets? Being rented out to greenhorns by some livery? If he was going to get shed of the horse at all, he wanted it to be to the right place, the right owner. Somebody who'd appreciate the horse's value and character.

He couldn't think of a soul in San Francisco who filled that bill. Besides, most folks here took the horse-drawn cabbies that were around every corner—he wouldn't wish that on any horse—or the cable cars that continually rolled the tracks up and down the city streets.

No, he'd decided just before they walked through the stable doors. He'd wait until they got to Seattle to decide.

The men readied their mounts, then went back to the hotel to pay up. And then Goose took them down to the dock to catch the ferry. Grover had bid them good-bye as they left the stable, and rode off to the east and Prescott. Slocum would miss Grover, and he imagined the others would, too. The last thing Slocum had said to him was "Don't get lost, now."

But he would, Slocum thought, and shook his head. That dang Grover always got lost.

Meanwhile, Smollets, traveling overland, was already halfway up the Oregon coast, according to his calculations. It felt good not to have a blasted horse to look after—or to up and die on him—and his arm was feeling better, too. The jail back in Sacramento had had a doctor come and look at it. He'd said the slug went all the way through, and there was no serious damage. Then he had wrapped Smollets's upper arm and shoulder and called it a day.

Smollets was still wearing the original dressing, but it didn't smell bad and he had stopped bleeding the second the doctor had sewed it up. It still gave him some trouble, but it was nothing he couldn't handle.

Actually, he felt he could handle nearly anything. He'd left Slocum and the rest of his pursuers clueless back in San Francisco, and now they'd never find him. Additionally, he currently had over two hundred dollars in the inner pocket of his fine, new suit, and a hideout gun secreted up his sleeve.

He felt like a new man.

It turned out that Goose hadn't booked them passage just to cross the Bay—he'd booked passage all the way to Washington State! Slocum was a little alarmed when he learned of it, but Goose assured him that the ship would get them there in slap time, and the passage for the horses wasn't that much. Of course, it was double for Slocum's two, but this didn't seem to cross Goose's mind.

So they busied themselves loading the horses—into what Slocum considered pretty shabby stalls, down in the cargo hold—and found their cabin. It was set up for two men, so they drew straws for the beds.

Slocum "won" the floor. Another reason to be unhappy. But the fact that the ship would get them to Seattle in less than two days—the wind being good—helped to soothe him somewhat.

The shipboard food was decent, if nothing special, and Slocum met another pretty girl. Didn't he always? He didn't sleep with this one, though, even though she proved quite willing. Her name was Diana, she was a virgin, and she was traveling with her mother. Which gave them no place to go, even if Slocum had wanted to. He just hadn't shaken Samantha out of his system yet.

So Diana had to settle for a little clandestine necking on the boat's stern, when her mother wasn't around.

They pulled into Seattle right on the time, and Slocum was the first one down to get the horses. He had learned that Kemo didn't like traveling by water and that Speck did. But both horses were aching to get off the boat and stretch their legs.

Goose and Xander were eager, as well. Goose was aching to see his Mariska and their kids. And Xander? Just because it was a new place, with people waiting for him. This was apparently a new experience for him, and Slocum felt for the kid.

Since the horses hadn't been ridden—or moved—for a couple days, Slocum elected to walk his through town. Goose and Xander followed suit, with Goose gabbing nonstop the whole time about his house and his wife and his girls and his boat.

"Where's it moored?" Slocum asked him. He hadn't seen any small craft back at the docks.

"Oh, we'll get there. Got my own private dock!"

Great. They were walking inland.

But after another block, Goose changed directions and headed them south, then, about a half mile later, headed them back east. Slocum was beginning to wonder if he'd let Goose hang around with Grover too long.

But they came out on a narrow beach, which, when they walked about a block or so down it, led to a dock and a sign that said, "FERRY." There was no ferry there, but, Slocum thought, at least it was promising.

While they sat with the horses—for which he was grateful, since his boots (and feet) were made for riding, not walking—Slocum looked across the water at what looked like a vast island, long and verdant with trees. He thought he smelled pines and fruit, too. Apples?

"Here comes the ferry!" said Xander, jumping to his feet.

Indeed, a rickety-looking ferryboat was rapidly closing on the dock where they were waiting. Actually, it was more of a large raft with a small structure in the center of it, and a wide deck all the way around with a rail you could tie horses to. There were a few scattered benches, too, probably in deference to any ladies willing to chance the ferry.

They paid twenty-five cents each, plus another twenty-five for each horse, and then, because they were the only passengers, the ferry shoved off.

The ferryman seemed to know Goose, since he was greeted with a jovial "Hey, Goose, how you doin'?"

"Fine, Clovis, just dandy, and thanks for asking."

Xander cleared his throat, waiting to be introduced.

Goose put an arm around the boy. "Clovis, I'd like you

to meet my son, Xander. Xander, this is Clovis Hitchens, who ferries the people and goods back and forth."

Clovis, a medium-sized man with dark hair, clapped his hands together and then shook both of Xander's enthusiastically. "A boy! Goose, you never told me you had you a boy! Pleased to meet you, Xander!"

"It's a long story, Clovis," Goose said, and Slocum, for one, was glad that he didn't launch into it on the spot. "And I'd also like you to meet my good friend, Slocum."

Slocum and Clovis shook hands, and Clovis said, "Hey, you ain't related to that Slocum in the dime books, are you? My kid reads those things all the time."

Before Slocum had a chance to reply, Goose said, "Hell, Clovis, he *is* that Slocum, honest to God."

"Well, I'll just be damned!" was Clovis's response. He needed to take a step toward the rail and grab it, lest he fall down. "Wait'll I tell my Jimmy!" He shook Slocum's hand again, pumping it more firmly this time. "I got a livin' legend ridin' my ferry!"

Slocum was about to thank him for adding "living" to the last sentence—and to argue the "legend" part—when the ferry pulled up to the dock on the other side. Clovis quickly tied it to the pilings, then helped them with the horses.

"Which one'a those spotted critters is yours, Mr. Slocum?" he asked.

"The two on the far end," Slocum said. "And it's just Slocum, no Mister. 'Less you're talkin' to my daddy, that is."

"Slocum. Yessir!"

"No 'sirs,' either, okay?"

Clovis looked, for a moment, like Slocum had struck him, but Goose must have signaled something to Clovis, because then he broke out in a grin again.

Slocum said, "You read those books, too? They're all lies, y'know."

Clovis shook his head. "I ain't much of a reader. Hell, I ain't no reader at all. But my Jimmy tells me about 'em."

Slocum grinned this time. "That how you knew I rode an Appy?"

Clovis shook his head again. "Nope. Goose, here, has been ridin' ol' Kip, here, as long as I've knowed him. And the other three all have spots."

Slocum laughed. It was obvious.

They got to the shore with little trouble, although Kemo was still a little jumpy from having to cross the water again, and Slocum said, "Where's your place, Goose? Don't seem like there's anything here but pine trees and ferns."

The place was lush with them, in fact. Slocum couldn't even see a path leading into the forest.

"Oh, it's just a little ways," Goose said, swinging a leg over Kip.

Slocum secured Speck's girth, then mounted up, too.

From behind them, on the ferry, Clovis shouted, "Kiss that pretty Mariska a'yours for me, Goose!"

Goose laughed and shouted back, "Not till I kiss her for myself!"

19

On the boat coming up from San Francisco, Goose had talked of little except his wife, Mariska, and his daughters: Katie, twelve, Annie, ten, and Sophia, seven. Katie was his own private stablehand. She'd been horse-crazy ever since she was big enough to crawl on all fours—and whinny. Annie was the artist in the family. Her drawings constantly graced their walls. And Sophia was their budding cook. She was only seven, but she'd learned to make a complete breakfast—from coffee to pancakes—and clean up after herself.

And now that he was on his home turf and they were following the shoreline south, Goose went on and on about the girls. Goose had talked them up so much Slocum figured that he was bound to hate them when they met. But Xander kept asking questions, goading Goose to tell him more and more, so much that Slocum was relieved when they turned from the beach onto a wide lane and started back into the woods, toward the house.

They reached it in a few minutes. It was a common-enough looking cabin, but somehow set up on stilts—so far as Slocum could figure. There were three stories to it, with a wide, wraparound veranda on the first level.

Slocum tried to take it all in, and all he could say was "Wow!" If this was what kind of money folks made selling fish, he was in the wrong business.

But Goose said, "Thanks. I'll tell my father-in-law that you liked it." He grinned, and kept on riding.

"It's his house?" Slocum asked. "I thought he was Russian. That he lived over there."

"Oh, he lives in Siberia, all right. He just lives here when he's in this country." Goose reined Kip down a side path, and the others followed. "We live down here."

Slocum could hear and smell the sea, but he couldn't see it. The trees were too thick. Again, the heady scent of apples fought its way through the overpowering scent of pine resin. Samantha would have loved this place, Slocum couldn't help but think.

"Here we are!" Goose exclaimed, as the grin that had been plastered over his face exploded into a look of unadulterated joy.

The path opened into a large clearing. Slocum could see that pasture land had been cleared, along with a large truck garden and a small field full of maturing corn. And then there was the house.

While Xander ooohed and aaahed, Slocum was struck speechless. The house was constructed of logs, tightly chinked, but this was no cabin. He figured it had to be at least two thousand square feet on the inside, and it was two stories tall, with a big stone chimney at each end, and one in the middle.

He was still staring when the front door burst open and three of the cutest little redheaded girls he'd ever seen popped out into the yard, all smiles and laughter, and ran first to Goose, then Xander.

Slocum didn't notice until after she was outside, but a beautiful woman had also stepped through the door. She was blond and statuesque, and her hair was pulled back into a bun. There was a green apron tied about her, and she was tossing a red and white checkered dish towel over her shoulder.

"Goose!" she cried, and ran to his arms.

While Goose introduced Xander to everybody, Slocum led all the horses over to the barn. It was a small affair, having only one stall, a tack closet, and a grain and hay room, which was hardly larger than the stall. The pasture would have to do. He just hoped that it wouldn't keep up raining. It had just started to patter on the tin roof.

One at a time, he led the horses inside and stripped them of their tack, then led them to the pasture gate. When he turned them loose, every one of them kicked up his heels and ran around, play-fighting and bucking and enjoying the rain and the freedom. Rain dripping from the brim of his hat, he stood there, watching and grinning, until he felt a hand touch his shoulder.

"Oh," he said. "Hey, Goose."

"Thanks for turnin' the horses out, buddy," he said. "Come on up and meet the family!" Twelve-year-old Katie tagged along behind him, but her eyes were on the horses. Goose's expression told Slocum that there hadn't been any of the nasty repercussions he'd feared about Xander. It appeared that the boy had been accepted, just like that.

Slocum was happy for him. Mariska could have justifiably made Goose's life hell for dropping news like that into her lap, but she hadn't. Slocum hadn't so much as met her yet, but he could already tell that he was going to like her.

"Are they Palouse horses?" Katie asked, without an ounce of shyness.

"Yes'm, they sure are," Slocum replied.

"They're beautiful!"

Slocum grinned. "I'd say thanks, but I didn't breed 'em. And the one farthest out, with the full blanket with lots of spots? That's your brother's gelding. His name is Eagle," he said, before she could ask.

Like a much younger child, she clasped her hands together and held them under her chin, grinning.

"And so everything is taken care of," Mariska said as she joined them at the table. She had made a feast for Goose's homecoming, and seemed to have taken into account that any son of Goose's would have inherited his appetite.

And she'd been right, naturally. The boy ate half a loaf of fresh-baked bread, all by himself.

Slocum had been expecting some sort of exotic Russian cuisine, but Mariska had obviously learned to cook in America. They had a huge roast of beef with potatoes and carrots and onions, coleslaw with plenty of onion, bread with butter and strawberry jam, creamed corn, steamed peas and onions. And for desert, she'd made two fat apple pies and a big pan of apple cobbler.

Apologetically, she said, "Sorry, no fish tonight."

And Goose said, "We have fish most every meal. This beef's a special treat!"

Mariska smiled. "I'm glad you're pleased."

Goose, grinning, reached for her hand and kissed it before he scooped himself up another slice of pie.

"My Mariska can out-cook your Samantha, I think, Slocum," he said.

Slocum didn't answer. He just smiled.

Xander filled the awkward void by saying, "You gotta come up and see my room, Slocum. I mean, you just gotta!"

Goose laughed. "Sure, he's gotta. It's our guest room, too."

Slocum's smile broadened. "I guess so, Xander." The boy leapt immediately to his feet, but, with a chuckle, Slocum waved him down again. "After dinner, son, after dinner."

Mariska laughed, too. "Just like his father," she said. "Always in a hurry."

"Somethin' we'd best be in a hurry about," said Goose, "is gettin' that barn made bigger. We gotta get Eagle in there, too."

Slocum suddenly had a terrific idea. "You'd best make it bigger than that, Goose."

"Why?"

"Because I'm givin' Kemo to your Katie."

Down at the other end of the table, Katie was so shocked that she fell off her chair and landed on the floor with a loud boom.

"Mr. Slocum!" Mariska gulped. "It's far too much to—"

Slocum waved his hands. "No, I insist. Goose's been tellin' me how much she loves horses, and Kemo needs a new home. I don't wanna sell him, lest he end up in bad circumstances. I'll feel a whole lot better knowin' that he's in the hands of Katie, here."

Goose, helping Katie back up and into her chair, said, "Slocum, that's about the nicest thing I—"

Slocum held up a hand again. "Nothin' to it, Goose. You folks'd be doin' me a favor." He meant it, too.

Katie had found her voice again, and said, "Mr. Slocum, thank you, thank you so very much! I can't, I mean, I don't, I mean . . ."

Slocum had to cut somebody off again. "That's okay, Katie, and you're welcome. You just have to promise to treat him right. Course, Xander'll be watchin', and see that you do." He took another bite of pie. "And that includes buildin' him a stall." He glanced at Goose and caught his eye. "A box stall, like Kip's got." He turned to Katie again. "All right?"

The girl had turned into one large smile. She said, "Yessir!"

Slocum smiled back. "And it's just Slocum, Katie. No 'Mister' to it."

Katie inched out of her chair to stand. "M— I mean, Slocum, may I ask a question?"

"Go ahead, Katie."

"May I kiss you?"

Slocum chuckled. "I reckon you can, Katie, I reckon so."

She ran around the table and threw her arms around his neck. "Oh, thank you, thank you, Slocum!"

Three rainy days later, the addition was completed. At one point, Mariska said that it was amazing what three men could turn into a decent-looking barn in three rainy days. And it *was* amazing. In addition to adding the new stalls, they had put in a second story, complete with a hay mow and chutes down which to drop hay to the horses.

Mariska had also laid claim to one end of the structure, moving the contents of the house's attic into it, and freeing up enough space so that Slocum now had his own room.

"Ain't no need," Slocum told her time and time again. "I'm fine and dandy campin' on Xander's floor!"

But she'd have none of it, and he ended up in a small, starkly appointed room with an actual bed and mattress. Which he greatly—if secretly—appreciated.

However, once the barn addition was finished, his feet started to itch. It was time he went wandering again. The reward money for catching Smollets—the first time—had come in, but Sheriff Black, down in Tucson, couldn't send it until the man had been caught again and was safely locked up and awaiting trial.

This put a bit of a crimp in Slocum's plans, especially since he'd spent a couple hundred dollars for the lumber, nails, and shingles for Goose's new addition. They'd all chipped in, of course, but Slocum would only take half of Xander's share, and instructed Goose to put it in the bank for his college fund.

He was bound and determined to get that boy educated.

Sensing Slocum's uneasiness, Goose invited him, on the fourth day, to take a ride with him into town. Slocum readily agreed, and the two, on Speck and Kip, took Clovis's ferry to the mainland and into town.

There was sure a lot more to Seattle than Slocum had seen on the way in! The town stretched out and upward, and the docks were immense. In the oldest part of town, saloons and brothels were everywhere, with the newer buildings being the farthest from the water and the docks. Slocum saw all manner of businesses, from tailors to furniture shops and coffee shops, from confectioners and butchers and bakers to millenary shops. If you wanted it, you could find it in Seattle.

And then there came the residential section, which had its share of mansions—it reminded him some of Denver, in fact—and its smaller, more common abodes.

Even Slocum had to say that it was a helluva place.

If only it didn't rain so much. He didn't believe that he'd been completely dry since he arrived, and then only in the privacy of his new bedroom. He liked to strip off all his clothes and sit in the rocker in front of the fire and just let himself evaporate.

He was looking forward to his bedroom and that fireplace as they turned around and started back through town, back past the houses and into the business district.

They were just coming up to the Cattleman's Bank when something—rather, someone—across the way caught Slocum's eye.

"Goose!" he hissed.

"What?" Goose rode up and reined in Kip next to Speck.

"Look over in front of the bank."

Goose did, and the fog lifted from his expression. "Well, I'll be a son of a—"

"—bitching bastard!" Slocum finished for him. He kneed Speck, who nearly leapt across the street. With Goose coming close behind him, he jumped off his horse to the hitching rail, then to the sidewalk, and lifted a very surprised Harvey Smollets up by his lapels.

Smollets seemed so taken aback that he didn't recognize Slocum at first. But when he did, he started up a ruckus such as Seattle only saw when the Russian trawlers all came to port on the same day.

"Murder! Help!" he shouted over and over.

But not for long. "Oh, shut your damn trap," Slocum growled, and slugged him in the jaw.

Smollets went limp.

"You got a decent jail in this burg?" Slocum asked Goose, as he hoisted Smollets over his shoulder.

20

The deputy was so startled that he spilled his coffee when Slocum pushed through the jailhouse door, carrying Smollets.

"Who . . . who . . . who . . . ?" the deputy stammered.

Goose, who brought up the rear and shoved Smollets's dangling feet through the door, said, "Howdy, Joe. Brought you a prisoner to babysit."

The deputy stared at Smollets, still passed out over Slocum's shoulder, and Slocum, looking brutish and pissed, and said, "Which one?"

"Smollets, of course!" growled Goose. "The little one. But don't let that fool you. He's been arrested three or four times in the last couple'a weeks, and escaped just as many. And he's killed folks, too!"

Slocum finally let Smollets slide to the floor, where he landed with a soft thud. "What he's tryin' to tell you, Deputy—"

"Call me Joe. Joe Token's the whole of it, but just call me Joe."

"Joe, then," Slocum said, with surprising patience.

151

"What Goose is tryin' to say is that this piece of shit I just dropped on your floor is Harvey Smollets, who's wanted in Arizona Territory for cattle rustling, murder, and breakin' outta jail, just to get started on it."

Slocum paused and Joe said, "I got a feelin' there's more . . ."

Goose then launched into the rest of the story, going from his injury—he took off his shirt to show Joe the results—to the trek across the desert and up the California coast, then the finding of Smollets "lying in wait" for them behind the corpse of a dead horse, the appearance of Marshal Grover . . .

"We sent for somebody with federal powers from Prescott," Slocum cut in.

"He's a U.S. deputy marshal. He came to cart Smollets back home to face charges, but he's on his way back to Prescott right now, ever since Smollets busted out of the Sacramento jail. But they'll send somebody else, won't they, Slocum?"

Slocum nodded. On the floor, Smollets was coming back to consciousness.

Slocum asked, "You got some place safe where we can stash him, Joe?" He quickly told of Smollets's history with jails and lawmen—and matrons.

The deputy got out of his chair again, and led Slocum, dragging Smollets, back to the cells, which were behind a locked door. This led them to an aisle with cells opening off either side. The cell block was currently empty, and Joe put Smollets in one of the center cells on the left side of the aisle. He locked the door, then escorted Goose and Slocum back to the office and locked the cell block door behind them, too.

"You goin' home past the Lister place, Goose?"

Goose looked up. "Yeah. You want me to send him on up?"

"Better," replied Joe, with a nod. "I want somebody back there with a loaded gun."

"Across the aisle," said Slocum. "And his meals get shoved to him with a broom handle or somethin'. Don't take *any* chances, no matter how stupid or unlikely you think they are."

"Check," Joe said. He sat down behind his desk and produced a piece of paper, which he shoved toward Slocum. "If you wouldn't mind fillin' that out?"

Slocum hated paperwork, but he sat down and filled it out without complaint, signed his name, then pushed it back toward the deputy. "That it?"

Joe took the paper, glanced over it, then stuck it in the top desk drawer. "John Slocum. Have I heard'a you before?"

Slocum shrugged, then pushed back his chair and stood up. "Possible. I get around."

"Huh," said Joe, then tilted his head to one side and shrugged again. "Guess that's it, then. You fellers can go. But you might want'a check back with me in a couple, three days."

Goose tipped his hat. "Thanks a lot, Joe. My best to your Sandra and the kids."

Joe nodded. "You've got it, Goose. Same to Mariska and the girls."

Goose popped out in an enormous grin. "And boy. Found out I had me a son. Had him for sixteen years and didn't know it!"

Joe smiled wide, stood up, and stuck out his hand toward Goose, who shook it. "Well, congratulations! Bring him around sometime soon! What's his name?"

"Name's Xander. Xander Martin," Goose said, adding his last name with pride.

"For Alexander?"

"Yeah."

"Well, congratulations again, Goose. Couldn't happen to a nicer fella."

Slocum remained silent. But he agreed, he agreed all right.

Back at Goose's place, they put the horses up in their new lodging. Kemo had had the stall all day, so Slocum turned him out in the pasture and put Speck inside. Kemo, at least, enjoyed the mud, rolling and generally making a mess of himself. He figured that little Katie wasn't going to be real happy with him, but too bad. He was too tired out to care.

Goose had stopped to tell everybody he knew about the recapture—make that the re-re-recapture—of Smollets, including Clovis, during the ferry ride. And now Slocum was preparing to hear him tell it all over again to Mariska and Xander. He hoped the girls were in the house, too, so that Goose could get it over with all at once. He didn't know if he could take it yet again.

He was in luck.

Everybody was home, and everybody had time to sit at the table and hear Goose relive the thrilling capture—according to him, anyway—of Smollets, and his current incarceration in the local jail.

At least Slocum imagined that he covered that. To be frank, he fell asleep in his chair somewhere during the part where he and Goose took Smollets to jail.

"Slocum?" Somebody nudged him in the ribs. It was Goose. "Slocum, is it gettin' borin' for you?"

Slocum grunted something noncommittal, then opened his eyes all the way. The whole damn family was staring at him. "Sorry, Goose, Mariska," he said. "And the rest of you," he added.

Nobody said a word until he asked, "What's for supper?"

And then everybody started talking at once. It seemed that while he and Goose were gone to town, Xander had

had a little adventure of his own. Assured by Goose that he and Goose's father-in-law owned the whole southern half of the island, Xander had gone hunting. He'd brought down a decent-sized buck, which he'd brought home, skinned, and dressed out, and there'd be venison for dinner. Mariska and the girls had helped to carve up what they wouldn't eat today and tomorrow, and it was currently hanging in the smokehouse.

Goose went to Xander and pounded the boy on the back. "Good job! That's my boy!" he said, with all the pride of a father.

Xander looked pretty proud himself, Slocum thought, but he thought he'd best remind him to go easy on the venison shooting. This was a small island, and it was hard to tell how many deer were on it.

But Goose beat him to it, adding the promise to take Xander to the boat tomorrow and let him look it over.

Xander was plainly excited, and remained so throughout the dinner—venison steaks, mashed sweet potatoes with fresh butter and sour cream, fried onions, fresh baked bread, garden peas, and a giant vanilla layer cake, with raspberry frosting, for dessert—and until bedtime.

Slocum would have bet that Xander was dreaming of standing on the prow of the ship with a bowl full of fried onions in his lap. They'd been his favorite during dinner.

Slocum's, too.

But Slocum's dreams were erratic and interrupted. He was worried about Smollets, who was the last person on this earth that he'd want to be dreaming about. He couldn't even turn his thoughts to Samantha without Smollets butting in.

He finally gave up at about five in the morning and crept downstairs. To his surprise, he found Goose sitting beside the still-warm hearth.

Goose said, "You couldn't sleep either?"

Slocum nodded.

"Smollets?"

Slocum nodded again. "I ain't gonna get a good night's sleep until he's in the hands of the marshals and outta the state."

"Ditto," replied Goose. "I'm thinkin' that maybe, soon as it gets light out, we oughta go over to the jail and check on things."

Slocum nodded. "I think you're right. And I also think that one'a us should stay with him till he gets picked up."

Goose nodded.

Slocum added, "I'll stay today. You go ahead and take Xander out to the boat. I know he's really lookin' forward to it."

Goose smiled. "Okay. I'll spell you late this afternoon, then?"

"Fine by me. I say we take ten-hour shifts or so. Fine with you?"

"Sounds fair," said Goose. "It won't be for long, I don't imagine. Those Arizona marshal folks seem to be pretty much on the ball."

"Yup." Slocum couldn't think of anything more to say, and apparently neither could Goose. The two of them sat there, watching the last coals of the fire grow black and go out until the full dawn was upon them.

Smollets was wakeful, too, although he gave no outward sign of it, other than his narrowly cracked eyelids at the edge of his blanket. In the cell across from him was another deputy, to whom he had not been introduced.

This one had a Sharps rifle lying across his lap as he dozed in his chair. He'd brought a rocking chair along, telling the first deputy—Joe was the name, he thought—he was too liable to fall asleep if he lay down on the cot.

Smollets could have told the pantywaist that there was nothing to fear about the cots. His, at least, was the least conducive to sleep of any bed he'd ever lain upon.

They hadn't given him an opening for escape, yet. They put his meal tray on the floor and poked it toward him with a broom handle, of all things. If he asked for water, one of them had him stand in his cell—at gunpoint—while the second one poured water into his tin cup through the bars.

It made one feel like a zoo animal.

But he was confident that he'd think of something, some trick that hadn't crossed their minds, and had yet to cross his. The bottom line was that he wasn't going to trial, period.

He wasn't going to prison, or to be hanged.

He was going to live a free and prosperous life, the one he had always imagined. And he wasn't going to do it around here.

He closed his eyes in defiance, and tried to think happy thoughts. He also imagined himself escaping.

It crossed his mind that he didn't give a whit how many people he had to kill or shoot or maim to do it. He just knew he had to be free. And he was going to be.

Period.

21

Goose and Slocum showed up at the jail at about six o'clock, waking a dozing Joe and a sound-asleep guard back in the cell block. Smollets was sleeping on his cot, and didn't stir while the men traded places.

Goose hadn't had to come, but he had anyway. "Just in case," he'd said. Slocum was halfway relieved that he'd come along. If Smollets had made a break for it during the night, Goose's assistance would have been needed.

Joe, who was about to go off duty, listened to the men's plan and agreed with it, and later, while Slocum was locked back in the cell block with his rifle and his Colt and his cross-draw rig, he heard Joe explain it to the new man.

Later, the man—"Call me Ted. Ted White."—stuck his head back through the cell block door to introduce himself and make sure Slocum didn't need anything. Slocum didn't.

By that time, Smollets had come awake. When he saw the man sitting in the cell across the aisle from him, all he could do was growl.

Slocum smiled, although it was wholly unfriendly. "Guess you're in for it now, Smollets," he said.

Smollets muttered, "Bah!" and rolled over, his back to Slocum.

Which was fine with Slocum. He didn't want to stare at Smollets's ugly face any more than Smollets wanted to stare at his.

Deputy Ted came back around noon, scooted Smollets a tray using a broom handle, and asked Slocum what he'd like for lunch. There was a café around the corner, he said.

Slocum put in an order for a roast beef sandwich with plenty of mustard, fried potatoes, apple pie, and a thermos of coffee, and gave the deputy a dollar to pay for it. It wasn't more than ten minutes before he had it before him, and it was worth both the wait and the dollar. The sandwich was fat and full of good beef, and the fried potatoes were plentiful and crispy, and the apple pie came with a slice of cheddar on the side. He'd figured he was taking a chance, ordering beef in a seaside town, but he was glad he'd taken it. He'd never had fish and chips before, but the deputy recommended it highly. He was already planning on it for his dinner.

The day passed without incident, other than the deputy's report that U.S. marshals were coming up from Sacramento to take charge of the prisoner and move him to Prescott. That, and a telegram from Grover, who was back in Prescott again. He congratulated Slocum on the recapture of Smollets, and added that he only got lost once on the trip back.

Slocum chuckled at that. Grover may have only gotten lost one time, but it probably took him from the western slope of the Rockies to some place in northern Nevada.

Goose showed up promptly at six o'clock, just as Slocum was finishing his fish and chips—delicious, but not so filling as the beef had been—and after telling Slocum all about Xander's reaction to the ship and mentioning, in passing, that it had stopped raining, Goose switched places with Slocum, with Slocum promising to replace Goose at six in the morning.

When the deputy—Joe, again—let him out of the cell block, he announced that the marshals ought to pull into town around tomorrow, midday. "They're comin' in on the *Cindy Lou*," he said. "She's always right on time."

"Thanks," replied Slocum with a tip of his hat. "I'll be glad to be shed of him." He meant it, too. In spades.

When he got outside, he found Xander, waiting on Eagle. "Pa figured you might get lost, so I came along to show you the way back," he said brightly. Then apologetically, "Not that you need showin'. But Pa . . ."

Slocum waved his hand, then checked Speck's girth and swung up on him. "Did he say you couldn't take any detours on the way back?"

Xander grinned. "Not a word."

Slocum nodded, and reined Speck away from the rail. "Good. Where's the nearest saloon?"

They located Beck's Saloon, which looked like a fairly decent place, and went inside. Slocum was sick of quirlies, and ordered himself the best cigar in the place. He was right—they had them. He would have liked to celebrate the imminent transfer of Smollets with a glass—or a bottle, more like—of champagne, but he decided to hold off on that until Smollets was really and truly gone.

He settled for bourbon instead.

Xander settled for a beer.

When they arrived back at Goose's house, Slocum found out that Mariska had kept his dinner warm. He almost told her that he'd eaten, but when she told him what she was holding for him—roast venison, a baked potato, fresh peas, and fresh bread—he decided that two suppers had never hurt anybody.

Xander joined him, and they both shoveled in the food

like there was no tomorrow, while an animated Xander told him about his visit to Goose's boat.

"Boat" wasn't really the word for it. According to Xander, it was more like a ship or a schooner. Xander described the beams and masts and sails, the upper and lower decks, and the crow's nest: Xander had climbed up to the top, and he said he could see for miles and miles.

Slocum said, "I'm gonna have to get you or Goose to take me to see the ship, too. She sounds like she's somethin' to see!"

Actually, Slocum had a sliver of knowledge when it came to ships and the sea. He'd once set sail on the high seas—he was knocked unconscious in a bar fight, then rolled and shanghaied—and got all the way to Panama before he had a chance to jump ship and make his way back up to the States.

He couldn't say he was a fan of the sea, so to speak, but he admired the men who made a living sailing it, and the boats in which they traveled the waters. And now he was even more impressed with Goose, too. A ship was a whole different kettle of fish (so to speak) than a boat. He wondered if Goose's father-in-law had had something to do with its acquisition.

"Well, I'm impressed," he said, cutting off Xander's lengthy speech about the mainsail.

"You'll be even more impressed when you see her," the boy said. "She's a real beaut, Slocum!"

"Sounds like it," Slocum said, grinning.

"Oh! I forgot to tell you her name. She's the *Mariska*. Isn't that nifty?"

Slocum ruffled the boy's hair, then glanced up at Mariska. She was staring at Xander and smiling. It seemed that she'd fallen in love with him. Oh, she'd been welcoming from the first, but Slocum was surprised at the depth of genuine affection in her eyes.

It just affirmed Slocum's previous conclusion: Xander

had fallen into the best of all possible worlds. And best of all, they wanted him there.

By nine-thirty that evening, Slocum was sound asleep out at Goose's house. Goose had fallen asleep, too, and sat, dozing, in the jail's rocking chair, his rifle angling to rest nose-down on the floor beside him. He was snoring lightly.

Across the aisle, in the opposite cell, sat Harvey Smollets, cross-legged on his cot, working steadily but quietly on something he held hidden in his lap.

It was almost a key. Well, it would be close enough when he was finished. And he had to get it very close to get out of his cell without waking Goose or the deputy. At least, he assumed there was a deputy on duty. Smollets hadn't seen him—nor had he heard a peep—since he'd taken the dinner tray away.

Smollets had kept the spoon, the handle of which he'd flattened surreptitiously beneath one leg of his cot. Next, he'd flattened the top by slowly rubbing it against the stone wall at the back of his cell. Amazing that they'd use real silver flatware for a jail, he thought. Not only was it expensive, but it was soft and malleable.

Next, he had to create the teeth—not as difficult as it sounded, especially if one had once worked for a locksmith, which Smollets had, in his youth. And it was helpful to have handy the rough-cut granite wall at his rear.

He'd seen the key the guard used to lock him up. It was nothing but an old skeleton key, the kind that would open nearly anything. He hoped so, anyway, because by ten o'clock, he had fashioned a reasonable facsimile.

Goose was still snoring, although more loudly now than before.

As quietly as possible, Smollets rose from his cot and tiptoed across the cell, to the door. His hand through the bars, he located the keyhole, said a quick, silent prayer, and slipped his homemade key into the opening.

It took him a few minutes to situate the key just right—his former spoon was a good deal less thick than their old iron key—but he finally got it.

A satisfying *click* came to his eager ears.

He looked up quickly to make sure that Goose hadn't stirred, then quietly let himself out of the cell, silently closed the door behind him, and tiptoed toward Goose.

Goose didn't wake up that night, primarily because Smollets smashed him in the temple with the butt of his rifle, which was just about to slip from his fingers. Smollets had to move fast to keep him from tumbling from his chair, and then he relieved him of his sidearm, as well, and arranged him to look as natural as possible.

That accomplished, he shoved the Colt pistol through his pants belt, quietly lifted the rifle, and crept toward the cell block door. He peeped through the small, barred window in it and saw . . . nothing. No one.

Either no one was on duty, or else the man who was had gone out to do rounds. A look at the clock told him the latter was most likely.

His makeshift key worked on the cell block door, too. *All hicks are morons,* he told himself as he crept out into the office, then to the front door. He wasn't so lucky there. He managed to slip out the door and around the corner, into the alley, just before the deputy spotted him. Still, he stood in the alley for several minutes, shaking right down to his shoes, before he headed up the street, keeping to the shadows, toward a livery he'd spotted in the days before that bastard, Slocum, spotted him outside the bank.

The livery was locked, but he fell back on old tricks: he let himself in through a stall window and found himself a plain horse. He had it saddled and ready to go in no time at all, and let himself out the back door.

In no time at all, he was galloping through the forest, and well clear of Seattle.

22

Dawn broke, and with it, Slocum rose. Since he was up before the family, he quietly dressed and went down to the barn, to saddle Speck and ride out to the ferry.

"First fare of the day?" he asked Clovis when the ferryman came across to pick him up.

"Yessir, that you are, Slocum. Where's Goose this mornin'?"

"Still at the jail, waitin' for me to relieve him."

Clovis nodded his head. "Oh, yeah. He's babysittin' that prisoner, ain't he?"

Slocum nodded. "That he is. And he's gonna be pretty damn sick of it by the time I show up to relieve him."

Clovis laughed. "That Goose! He's a character, ain't he?"

Slocum agreed that Goose was, and very nearly told the ferryman that he, Clovis, was a real fruitcake, too. But he didn't. He'd probably have to cross this stretch of water at least a couple more times before he left, and he didn't want to swim it.

Clovis let him off at the opposite dock, and after Slocum

disembarked, he swung up on Speck and made his way into town.

Seattle was just waking up, and he noticed a knot of people standing at the front of one of the livery stables, arguing about something. He didn't pay much attention.

He stopped at the sheriff's office, tied Speck at the rail, gave a last rub to his neck, then went inside.

Joe was dozing at the desk, and it took Slocum a couple of throat clearings to wake him. "How's the prisoner?" Slocum asked, once Joe was capable of speech.

"Fine. Least, I ain't heard a peep outta him," Joe replied sleepily.

As he slowly got to his feet and headed toward the cell block door, Slocum asked him, "Ain't you boys got a sheriff, or you just hire a bunch of deputies 'cause you can pay 'em less?"

This got a laugh from Joe, who then explained that the sheriff was in Spokane, on business. Slocum nodded, and Joe stuck the key in the lock. "Rise and shine!" called Slocum as the door swung open.

But Goose didn't budge. Slocum went to him, slapped his cheeks and tried to bring him around, but all Goose could do was groan. Joe, who was the first to notice Smollets's absence, yelled, "Hang on!" to Slocum, then hotfooted it out of the jail and up the street without another word.

Slocum couldn't help Goose, at least not till a doc showed up and figured out what the hell was wrong with him, so he explored Smollets's cell. He found the remains of the scraped-off spoon on the granite wall, and traces around the keyhole to the cell.

He could just about imagine how it went down. Goose had fallen asleep. Smollets had swiped a piece of silverware from his own dinner tray, and once Goose was sawing logs, he'd been able to grind it into shape on the granite wall.

The crafty little shit!

Slocum would be on his trail, all right, just as soon as he talked to a doctor about Goose.

Joe was back sooner than Slocum had thought possible, with both the doctor and another man in tow. The doctor went right to work on Goose, shooing Slocum out of the cell block with Joe and the other man, who was ranting and carrying on about something.

The subject of his ravings didn't strike Slocum until he'd been out front for a few minutes. The man was from the livery up the street, and someone had broken in during the night and stolen one of his client's horses.

"How many times have I told you, Sam, you need to hire a night watchman for that place?" Joe asked before Slocum had a chance to get a word in edgewise.

"Smollets" was all he said, and they both turned to look at him. "How'd he get in?" he asked.

"Crawled in through one of the blamed stall windows!" shouted the hostler, whom Joe had been calling Sam.

"He take a plain-colored horse?" Slocum asked.

"Plain chestnut, no white," said Sam, and wrinkled his forehead.

"Let himself out the back way?"

Sam pulled himself up to his full height, which was almost to Slocum's chin. "You in on this deal, mister? How come you know so blamed much? Arrest him, Joe!"

Calmly, Slocum turned toward the deputy. "Same trick he pulled down in Sacramento. He's probably goin' east. He'd have taken a boat, otherwise."

Sam tried to butt in again, but Joe told him in no uncertain terms to sit down and shut up.

He did, looking surprised.

"What's the doc say?"

Slocum shook his head. "Don't know yet. But I think it's bad. He threw me out."

Joe scratched the back of his head. "I'll be damned if I can figure out how Smollets got himself out of that cell!"

"He made a key."

"What?"

"Go take a look at that granite block wall at the back of his cell. He's been grindin' something silver against it."

The deputy slumped into his desk chair. "Aw, dammit, anyhow! I been tellin' the sheriff we need to get those cells re-keyed!" He held up an old-fashioned skeleton key, black and rusty. "One opens everything in the whole damn place. Hell, one'll open half the locks in town!"

"You got a lot of trusting folks in this town," Slocum observed.

"Too trusting." The deputy shot a glance Sam's way. "We try to clean up the messes, but we can't catch pie thieves when the pie gets set in a window to cool."

Slocum added, "Along with a little sign that says, 'Take me, I'm delicious.'" He shook his head.

"Excuse me?" They all turned toward the voice. It was the doctor, standing in the cell block entrance.

"How's he doin', Doc?" Slocum asked immediately—and hopefully.

"Well, whoever hit him busted his skull, all right. He was just lucky it wasn't a fraction of an inch lower, or he might never wake up. As it is, he'll likely be unconscious for a day or so. Got to wait until the swelling goes down in his brain. And then he's gonna have to wear a helmet for a while, till the bones of his head have a chance to knit together."

Slocum heaved a tremendous sigh of relief, then sat down hard on a bench near the far wall. "Thank God," he breathed. He realized he'd grown to love old Goose like a brother over these last few weeks.

"He's a lucky man," said Joe, absently toying with his badge. "Lucky, lucky."

"What about my client's horse?" demanded Sam. "What am I supposed to tell him?"

"Doubt you could tell your client's horse a damn thing, since he's probably up in the Rockies by now," Slocum said. He couldn't resist.

Sam shot to his feet. "You know what I mean!"

Deputy Joe closed his eyes for a moment and shook his head. "Will everybody just shut the hell up?"

Sam sat down again, still seething. Slocum just shrugged. Then he sat forward and looked over at Joe. "I'd best go tell Goose's wife and kids," he said, and Joe nodded. Slocum figured he was relieved that there was one less thing he'd have to do.

"I'll wait for the marshals before I cut out after Smollets," Slocum continued as he stood up and took a last look in at Goose. He was sleeping peacefully.

"I'll be back," Slocum said, and left.

After he performed the difficult task of informing Mariska and the kids of Goose's condition, he began to make his plans. Xander was determined to tag along, and at first Slocum refused, mostly on Mariska's account. She had already nearly lost her husband—twice—to Smollets. She didn't want to lose a son to him as well, even if she'd barely known him for a week.

But in the end, they both had to relent. The boy was dead set on going along, and nothing either of them could do or say could dissuade him.

At about one, both Slocum and Xander said their goodbyes and set out for the ferry. They didn't have to wait long for Clovis to show up, and he got them across the water to the mainland in slap time. Next, they went to the jail, where they waited only a half hour for the federal marshals from California to show up.

Slocum and Xander both looked in on Goose while they

were waiting. His condition was unchanged, but at least it wasn't worse. Xander kissed his cheek and whispered something into his ear, and Slocum was touched.

When the marshals showed up, Slocum listened to Joe explain the situation to them. And when he walked out front, they introduced themselves.

One was tall and thin, and the other was shorter and a tad more portly. The tall, thin man stuck out his hand. "How do," he said, in a baritone voice. He had dark hair and a chiseled, clean-shaven face, and Slocum would have bet he had to beat the women off with a club. "I'm Deputy U.S. Marshal Ivan Greene. Call me Ivan."

The shorter marshal stepped forward. "And I'm Pete Rawlings. You can call me Pete. Glad to meet you, Mr. Slocum," he said in a surprisingly tenor voice. He had sandy hair and a thick handlebar mustache.

Slocum shook both their hands in turn. "Glad to meet you Ivan, Pete. Just call me Slocum. No 'Mister.' And this eager young lad is Xander Martin. He's the son of the man who got his head caved in last night."

Both marshals conveyed their sympathies.

Slocum continued, "He was also in on the recapture we made down in California, and he's comin' along."

Ivan narrowed his eyes. "Now, I don't know about that . . ."

"Try and talk him out of it, if you've got a spare day or two. Me, I'm settin' out after that murderin' son of a bitch."

The deputy marshals looked at each other, then at Slocum. "Okay. But you're in charge of the kid."

Xander protested, "I don't need nobody in charge'a me!"

But Slocum said brusquely, "Quiet." And the kid actually shut up!

To the marshals, Slocum said, "Let's move. He's got nearly a day on us. Don't know how well he knows the territory, but he can't know it any worse than me. Hope one'a you boys knows it better."

The four men galloped out of town, taking the main road and heading east, until the town was far behind them and the houses were replaced by trees and lush vegetation, verdant from the rain.

They were tracking a single rider now, a rider whose horse was missing a front right shoe and toed in. Slocum figured that Smollets was not only cruel, he knew *nothing* about horses except how to get on and get off, and how to use a whip to cut horseflesh.

The tracks slowed down, showing that the horse was traveling at a jog, then a walk, then a jog again, now that they were in the foothills. Slocum hoped to hell that the horse broke down before Smollets reached the mountains.

Not that he had anything against the horse: he just had a helluva lot against Smollets.

Both the marshals were decent trackers. At one point, where even Slocum lost the trail, Ivan picked it up. Of course, Ivan was where Slocum would have looked next. But it was handy to have four pairs of eyes looking when they didn't even have a game trail to follow.

23

They kept pushing until well after nightfall, but they still hadn't caught up with Smollets. They were still on his track, though. They made camp in a grove of apple trees, and Slocum settled back while Pete and Ivan rustled up some supper and Xander sat on a rock, staring out over the trail ahead.

Slocum figured that, the way they were traveling, they'd have at least another day before they came up against the mountains. He hoped to God they could catch Smollets before then. He didn't care much for mountain travel, or mountain survival, for that matter. It was too hard on the horses and too hard on him, now that he was getting older.

No, he thought, he'd take that back. Age had nothing to do with it. It was just hard, period.

He spoke up, breaking the silence. "When we get him, you boys are takin' him straight to Prescott, right?"

Ivan looked up from the fire. "Yessir. Course, Pete, here, wants to tie him to a tree and lash him bloody first, but I think that can be put off."

Pete looked up, too. "Oh, I do not, Ivan. You'd best quit tellin' people that, lest somebody believes you." He looked

173

over at Slocum. "He's always tellin' folks that. Scarin' 'em and stuff. I don't bite, mister."

Slocum snorted out a laugh. "Never said you did, Pete."

Pete jabbed a finger toward Ivan. "Well, *he* did."

"All right, all right, boys," Slocum said, standing. "Take it easy." The last thing he needed right now was an impending scuffle.

But before he got all the way up, Xander hissed, "Slocum! Come look!"

He made his way over to the boulder where Xander sat, and followed his pointing finger. About a half mile distant could be seen a soft glow: a campfire. Xander said, "I think he killed his horse already," which was exactly what Slocum was thinking.

He clapped Xander on the shoulder. "Your pop'd be proud of you," he said, then waved the others over while Xander basked in the glow of praise.

The others came to the same conclusion, and Ivan said, "Hot damn! Didn't think we'd catch him up this quick!"

Pete muttered, "I did. The way he was pushin' that poor horse . . ."

"Let's go get him," said Slocum, checking his guns.

"If you insist," Ivan said lackadaisically. "We get paid for the time we're out, y'know. Seems to me we could snatch him in the mornin' just as easy."

Slocum glowered. "That's what you think."

"We goin' in on foot, or are we takin' the horses?" Xander asked.

"On foot." Slocum was adamant. "The horses make too much noise."

"Aw, hell," said Ivan. "Let's go, then."

They walked the half mile carefully and quietly, despite Xander tripping over a log, then stepping in a gopher hole. "If you was a horse, we'd have to shoot you," whispered a grinning Ivan, helping him up.

"Only if I busted my leg," Xander snapped back, embarrassed.

"Quiet, you two!" Slocum hissed before starting forward again. The others followed.

They soon came to a little rise—the reason the light from Smollets's fire had been so dim—and lay down to peek over it. There sat Smollets, his back to them, in front of his fire.

His horse stood over to the left. Its head was down, and it held its right foreleg up off the ground. It was in obvious pain.

Slocum cursed beneath his breath. Didn't Smollets know to either shoot the critter—if the leg was broken—or bind it, if it wasn't? Apparently not. Judging from the nasty looks that Smollets threw the horse's way when it occasionally groaned, he didn't know shit.

Slocum wondered if he'd bothered to feed the horse, or even offer it water.

He doubted it.

Suddenly, at his right side, Pete brought up his rifle. "You're just gonna shoot him?" Slocum whispered.

"Yup," said Pete. "They changed the poster, in case it hasn't caught up with you yet. Now he's wanted, dead or alive."

The chestnut groaned again, and Smollets threw it another dirty look. The son of a bitch had given out on him mid-morning. He'd managed to lead it this far, hoping against hope that the stupid thing was just tired, but it hadn't gotten any better. Only worse.

He wondered if he should shoot it and just move on.

But dead things brought buzzards, and circling buzzards brought men. Men like that bastard Slocum. He had no wish to tangle with Slocum again. He just wanted to get the hell out of Washington State. Maybe up into Canada, although this was a poor time of year to think about moving north.

Here it was, only early October, and he was shivering in his jacket. He was also worried about bears. And cougars and wolves. But mostly grizzly bears.

No, he'd have to lead the horse again tomorrow. Perhaps he could shoot it at the edge of a cliff so that the body would tumble downward. That might throw any pursuers off the track.

Then again, perhaps not.

Goddamn horse! He picked up a rock and threw it at the chestnut's rump. It connected. Shocked, the gelding skittered to the side and almost went down. Smollets laughed aloud again. "Serves you right, you slab-sided—"

The slug reached him before the sound did. In fact, by the time the sound came to his ears, he was incapable of hearing it.

Or anything else.

Slocum lowered his rifle. He had stared at the body, watching for the slightest motion, long after the others were patting each other on the back. In the end, Pete hadn't taken the shot, or Ivan. They wanted him dead—or at least, they were the ones who had vocalized it—but it was Slocum's kill. And he took it.

Now Smollets was dead, and he wouldn't shoot at anybody else, wouldn't kill anybody else, wouldn't kill any more horses, and would rustle no more cattle from men who worked hard for a living.

Slocum always felt a little on the weasel side when he had to kill anyone—even when it was to save his own life, even when it was sanctioned by the law and common decency. But what was curious was that this time he didn't feel bad at all. Actually, he felt empowered.

It was bizarre.

"Shot smack through the head," called out Pete, who was checking the body. "I'll be damned if it didn't come out right in the middle of the bastard's forehead, too!" He looked at Slocum in admiration. "Nice shootin', Slocum!"

Slocum nodded, but his focus was on the chestnut. Xander finished going over the horse's foreleg, then stood up. "It ain't busted that I can tell," he said happily, and began to tear up one of Smollets's shirts into bandages. "It's sure swole up, though," he added.

The horse's bridle was just hanging round his neck. Smollets had obviously tossed it on him right over his halter. *Damned scum, in every sense of the word.* Slocum said, "Before you bandage him, feed and water him. I doubt Smollets bothered."

Xander nodded. He found water and gave some to the gelding, but could find no grain.

"I'm not surprised," Slocum said, pushing his hat back. "Well, just let him graze his way back to our camp when we go. That'll be something, anyway. And throw his saddle on him. It won't weigh that much to him, and the trail's kinda rugged."

Xander nodded. He was the one who'd fallen coming down.

"Ain't much to lug, is he?" Pete asked Ivan. Ivan had Smollets's head, Pete had his feet, and they were carrying him away from the fire. "Can you fellas grab his stuff?"

Slocum doubted that Smollets had anything of his own on him. Likely, it was all stolen. But he gathered it up anyway, stuffed Smollets's saddlebag full, then threw it over his shoulder.

"You got that leg all done?" he asked Xander.

"Yup."

"Okay, then." Slocum kicked out the fire. "Let's get back up with the rest."

"Slocum?"

"Yeah?"

"I didn't say nothin' before. You know, about the shot bein' so perfect and all, 'cause I know you value . . . what's

Mariska call it? The sanctity of life, I guess that's it." He looked away for a second, as if trying to figure out how to say something. Then he twisted back. He said, "Slocum, I'm sorry you felt like you had to be the one to do it, but I'm awful glad he's dead. Twice, he's nearly killed my pa."

Slocum hoisted the saddlebags with one arm and put the other around the boy's shoulders. "I know, Xander. It's all right to feel that way. Go ahead and revel in it, 'cause you ain't gonna have many more chances. To be happy that sorry turd's dead, I mean."

Xander nodded. He smiled a little. Then he clucked to the horse. "C'mon, ol' Red."

Slocum hurried to catch up. "That his name?"

Xander shrugged. "Don't know. But I figured it'd do till we get back to town. You gotta call him *some*thing."

"Yes, you do," replied Slocum, slowing again while the gelding paused to graze. "You've gotta call him something."

Back at camp, Slocum took off the bandages that Xander had applied to the stolen gelding's leg, then rubbed it down with liniment. He had to agree with the boy that the leg certainly didn't feel broken—unless it was a hairline fracture—but it was sure as hell sprained.

When he'd finished, he rebandaged it, then patted the horse on his neck. "Promise that tomorrow'll be easier, old son." The horse, grateful for attention, whickered softly.

Slocum and Xander went around the camp, pulling up grasses for him, too.

When they came back to the fire, Ivan handed Slocum a cup of coffee. "Ain't fresh, but it's hot," he said.

"Thanks." Slocum took a gulp. The heat felt good as it traveled down into his gut, and he was suddenly glad that he'd brought a blanket. This was the time of year he most liked to spend in Arizona or southern New Mexico. And he intended to get back down there as soon as humanly possible.

But first, he needed to get Xander back home and check on Goose.

Xander had already bedded down across the fire and his eyelids were drooping. "Night, Slocum," he said, in a half-asleep voice.

"Night, Xander," he replied.

Ivan and Pete were spreading out, too, and Slocum decided they had the right idea. He drained his coffee, stretched out on his blanket, and pulled the extra one over him. Then, using his saddle for a pillow, he went to sleep.

24

In the morning, Ivan pulled together enough sticks and branches to put together a travois, to take Smollets's body back to Arizona, and Pete idly watched him while he nursed a cup of coffee.

"Ain't you gonna help him?" Slocum asked. He had just finished making breakfast, and handed Pete a plate.

"Nope," said Pete, accepting it. "He's gonna make me pull the damned thing."

Slocum grinned and handed a plate to Xander, who was just waking up. Ivan took a break from making the litter when he was presented with breakfast, too. And Slocum sat down and joined them. He'd brought down several quail in the wee small hours, and put together a pretty decent stew—especially when it was served over slices of the good sourdough Pete had brought along.

When they finished breakfast, Xander cleaned up while Slocum checked Red, or whatever his name really was. The swelling seemed to have gone down some, and he was bearing weight on the leg. Slocum patted the gelding on the neck. "Good boy. Now we've gotta see how well you can hold up on the long walk into town. You think you're up for that, huh?"

"Oh, I think he'll make it all right," said Pete. Slocum looked over, halfway startled. He hadn't known Pete was there. "Thanks for the good breakfast, Slocum," Pete continued as he stepped closer to the horse. "I was out here before, lookin' at him. I think he's made of pretty tough stuff."

"Have to agree with you," said Slocum, nodding. The gelding grazed, paying them no mind, just happy to be away from Smollets.

Later, Xander and Socum bid good-bye to Ivan and Pete. And Smollets. As he had predicted, Pete's horse pulled the travois. And as Slocum had predicted, leading Red was slow going. The horse tried the best he could to keep up, but Slocum didn't want to strain him, which meant that they did a lot of stopping and starting. Xander didn't complain once, and Slocum was proud of him. He knew how much the boy wanted to get back and check on his father.

Slocum's mind was on Goose, too. Had he awakened, as predicted by the doctor? Or was he still on that cot in that cell, slumbering like Rip Van Winkle? Slocum hoped it was the former.

At least, as they neared the coast, the weather got a little better. There had been a light dusting of snow sometime during the night, and Slocum wasn't the least bit happy to see it when he woke. *Arizona,* he kept thinking. *Arizona.*

It was probably still in the nineties down in the valley.

He felt a little warmer just thinking about it.

Despite all the stopping and starting they did, they reached the edge of town at about nightfall, and went directly to the jail.

Joe was on duty again, and had good news for them. "Ol' Goose came out of it round ten this morning, hungry as a bear. We fed him good, had the doc come check him out, and the doc said he could go home. Course, he also said that he couldn't ride his horse or do any work for at least a month. That didn't make Goose too happy," he added with a grin.

Slocum smiled. "Good ol' Goose. He's a tough old bird, ain't he?"

"That he is, that he is," replied Joe.

Xander couldn't do anything but beam.

Goose was asleep when they arrived back on the island, but Mariska was delighted to have them back, and fed them apple pie while they—mostly Xander—told the story of catching Smollets. "So he's gone for good this time," Mariska said, looking relieved. "Thank the Lord."

Slocum had two pieces of pie to Xander's three—with homemade, hand-cranked ice cream—and by the time the boy was through telling the tale, Slocum wanted nothing more than to go to bed. Thinking fond thoughts of the soft bed and the fire that awaited him upstairs in the guest room, he excused himself from the table.

"I'll see Goose tomorrow, Mariska," he said. "But right now, I'm about to fall down."

They'd left Red—whose real name turned out to be Sundancer—at the livery, and Slocum had turned Speck out into the pasture. Because of their slow pace coming home, the gelding was still raring to go, and Slocum figured to let him work it out in the open. He'd been right. The second he stripped the tack from him and set him loose in the open pasture, Speck went from a standing start right into a full gallop, and circled the pasture three times before he came back to see what was for dinner.

He was a card, all right.

Slocum had also checked in on Kemo. Young Katie had been taking care of him, all right. He was brushed clean as a whistle, and there was plenty of hay in his manger. The old, familiar, soft and kindly look had come back into his eyes, too.

Slocum mounted the stairs and said a last good night to Goose's family, then climbed up to his guest room. He thought he'd leave tomorrow, maybe the day after, depending on whether there was any work Mariska needed done around the place.

After all, Xander was just a kid. He couldn't do everything.

He lit the fireplace, sat beside it for a while to get the chill out of his bones, then climbed between the sheets of his bed.

Within five minutes, he was asleep.

Ivan and Pete must have run across another town the day before, because the next midday, a boy came to the island from the telegrapher's office, bearing vouchers for Goose, Xander, and Slocum for the capture of one Harvey Smollets, alias Ned Spelling, alias Theodore Small, and on and on.

The reward was greater than Slocum had expected, and Xander was so excited he could barely contain himself. Goose hadn't woken yet, so they filled the time by going down to the mainland docks, where Xander proudly showed Slocum his father's ship.

"Whoa!" said Slocum, when Xander first pointed it out. It was big enough to be a whaler.

Xander took him aboard and showed him this and that, including the captain's quarters—filled with all things Goose-like—and the crew's, the mess hall and the vacant storage and chilling bins. Slocum was struck by the enormity of them. He'd been picturing a rowboat, for some reason, but instead, countless masts towered overhead, and other than the life rafts, there wasn't an oar in sight.

"What kind of fish does your dad go out after?" he asked Xander. "Tuna? Halibut? Squid, maybe?" He couldn't remember, off the top of his head, which fish came from which ocean.

Xander shrugged. "I dunno. I forgot to ask him."

Slocum grinned. The kid was no better informed in the ways of the sea than he was. Oh, well.

"You wait, though, Slocum," Xander continued. "He says I can go out with him on his next run. I'll learn it all, from cabin boy up!"

Slocum put his arm around Xander's shoulders. "I bet you will, kid. You're smart, and you're a quick study. I think you oughta fish with your pa until you've got enough money saved, and then you go back east to college. Or maybe San Francisco. They might be buildin' one any day. Then you can come back home and really be a help to your pa."

"But I don't wanna go to school!"

"Trust me, you'll like it," Slocum said with a grin. "'Sides, lots of pretty fillies around, and they love those college boys."

Xander rolled his eyes, and Slocum chuckled. "C'mon, kid, let's get us some lunch."

After they ate, Slocum stopped by the bank and cashed in his voucher for Smollets. He made Xander deposit his in the savings account Slocum had opened for him. The kid protested, but Slocum insisted. "You're gonna need that money someday for something important. Best start sockin' it away while you've got it. Besides, you've got money left from Arizona, don't you?"

Xander shrugged. "Couple hundred, I guess. Maybe more. Maybe two-fifty?"

Slocum hoisted a brow good-naturedly. "Boy, you're keepin' the candy merchants in business, single-handed, ain't you? Well, c'mon. You'd best stock up before we go back to Goose's."

"Yessir!"

Goose was awake and sitting up in bed when they got back to the house. But Mariska refused to let him get up and go down the stairs again, so she had fixed him a monumental lunch tray.

While he stuffed himself on sauteed venison with onions, mushrooms, and leeks, Xander excitedly told him about his and Slocum's visit to the "boat."

"It was real impressive, Goose," Slocum got in. "Don't know why you didn't introduce yourself as 'Captain'!"

Goose waved a hand, dislodging the forkful of potato salad he'd just scooped up and had halfway to his mouth. "Sorry, honey," he said as Mariska went to wipe it off the wall. "Now, Slocum," he went on, "I ain't just a captain. I own that boat. An' I didn't wanna brag."

Slocum laughed. "Goose, you're plumb full of surprises, that's all I can say."

Goose chuckled back at him. "That's me, all right."

"By the way, if you're feelin' up to snuff, and if there ain't anything I can do for Mariska, I believe I'll be gettin' on my way in the morning."

"But—" said Goose.

"It's too cold and too wet up here for these old bones," Slocum said. "I gotta get back down south, if Mariska's got no use for me."

"We'd love to have you stay the whole winter, Slocum," she said. "Not to work. Just as our guest."

"That's real nice, Mariska. Might be droppin' in on you sometime in the future, if you don't mind." He had grown fond of the whole family. "Now, I hope you don't mind, Goose, but I cashed out your voucher and put the money in your savings account. Figured you'd rather know where it was than hold that voucher out here at your place."

"I still say you don't owe me a dime'a that money, Slocum. I was just glad we got him. And you're welcome anytime. You know that."

"There you go again, Goose," Slocum said with a grin. "Too late now!"

"Slocum, you did exactly the right thing," Mariska cut in. "Why, that little . . . weasel! Two times he nearly killed my Garland!"

Slocum hoisted a brow. "Garland?"

Mariska suddenly turned beet red. Goose grimaced, then lowered his voice. "Don't tell nobody, Slocum. Okay?"

Slocum sat up straight and crossed his heart. "Hope to die, Goose."

"Thank God." Goose sighed, then turned to Mariska. "What we got for dessert, honey?"

WLODC 2009

Watch for

SLOCUM AND THE MEDICINE MAN

367th novel in the exciting SLOCUM series
from Jove

Coming in September!